If Katina had needed a warning that Zach was dangerous, the slow, predatory half smile that left his eyes cold would have provided it.

The gesture was casual. His hand did not even make contact with the skin of her cheek, but it was close enough for her to feel the warmth. She swayed away from it, but warning or not, she had no facility to prevent the image that surfaced in her head. It was a very specific image, sensory in its strength, long brown fingers moving over pale... She escaped the image in her head before she fell over, her breath leaving her parted lips in a raspy gush.

Well, that couldn't be good, could it?

Shame rushed through her as she lifted her chin. There was no way she was going to add herself to the long list of women who had made fools of themselves over Zach Gavros. For starters, she had too much self-respect, and second, a much too strongly developed sense of self-preservation.

Kim Lawrence lives on a farm in Anglesey with her university-lecturer husband, assorted pets who arrived as strays and never left, and sometimes one or both of her boomerang sons. When she's not writing, she loves to be outdoors gardening or walking on one of the beaches for which the island is famous—along with being the place where Prince William and Catherine made their first home!

Books by Kim Lawrence

Harlequin Presents

One Night with Morelli
Surrendering to the Italian's Command
A Ring to Secure His Crown
The Greek's Ultimate Conquest
A Cinderella for the Desert King
A Wedding at the Italian's Demand

One Night With Consequences

A Secret Until Now
Her Nine-Month Confession

Wedlocked!

One Night to Wedding Vows

Seven Sexy Sins

The Sins of Sebastian Rey-Defoe

Visit the Author Profile page
at Harlequin.com for more titles.

Kim Lawrence

A PASSIONATE NIGHT WITH THE GREEK

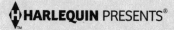

Recycling programs
for this product may
not exist in your area.

ISBN-13: 978-1-335-47856-6

A Passionate Night with the Greek

First North American publication 2019

Copyright © 2019 by Kim Lawrence

Printed in U.S.A.

HARLEQUIN®
www.Harlequin.com

A PASSIONATE NIGHT
WITH THE GREEK

CHAPTER ONE

Zᴀᴄʜ ʜᴀᴅ ʀᴇᴄᴇɪᴠᴇᴅ the message he had been waiting for while he was stuck in traffic. Sometimes a first-hand knowledge of the back streets of Athens, combined with a flexible attitude to rules, came in useful.

Zach possessed both.

For some of his formative years he had lived by his wits on those streets, finding it infinitely preferable to living with the grandmother who had resented having her daughter's bastard foisted on her, and the drunken uncle who had perfected bullying into an art form.

It took him just under half an hour and a few probable speeding fines to reach the hospital. He remained oblivious to the covetous stares that followed his long-legged progress from his car and through the building. It took him three more minutes to reach the intensive care unit where Alekis Azaria had spent three days in a medically induced coma after being successfully resuscitated following his last cardiac arrest.

Zach, as the closest thing the older man had to either friend or family, had been there the previous day when they'd brought him out of the coma. Despite the warnings that he had chosen not to hear, he had fully anticipated that Alekis would simply open his eyes.

The consultant had explained this sometimes happened but admitted there was a possibility that Alekis might never wake up.

Given the fact that the Greek shipping tycoon's presence here was on a strict need-to-know basis, it was no surprise that the same consultant who had issued this gloomy prognosis was waiting for him now, at the entrance to the intensive care unit.

The medic, used to being a figure of respect and authority, found himself straightening up and taking a deep steadying breath when the younger, tall, athletically built figure approached.

Zach didn't respond to the older man's greeting; instead, head tilted at a questioning angle, he arched a thick dark brow and waited, jaw clenched, to hear what was coming.

'He has woken and is breathing independently.'

Impatient with the drip-feed delivery Zach could sense coming, he cut across the other man, impatience edging his deep voice.

'Look, just give it to me straight.'

Straight had never been a problem for Zach. His ability to compartmentalise meant personal issues did not affect his professional ability.

'There seems to be no problem with Mr Azaria's cognitive abilities.'

A flicker of relief flashed in Zach's dark eyes. Intellectual impairment would have been Alekis's worst nightmare; for that matter it would have been his own.

'Always supposing that he was fairly...*demanding* previously?' the doctor tacked on drily.

Zach gave a rare smile that softened the austere lines of his chiselled, handsome features, causing a passing pretty nurse to walk into a door.

'He is accustomed to being in charge. I can see him...?'

The cardiologist nodded. 'He is stable, but you do understand this is early days?' he cautioned.

'Understood.'

'This way.'

Alekis had been moved from a cubicle in the intensive care unit to a private suite of rooms. Zach found him propped up on a pile of pillows. The events of the last week had gouged deep lines in the leathered skin of his face and hollowed out his cheeks, but his voice still sounded pretty robust!

Zach stood in the doorway for a moment, listening, a smile playing gently across his firm lips.

'Have you never heard of human rights? I'll have your job. I want my damned phone!'

The nurse, recovering her professional poise that had slipped when she'd seen Zach appear, lifted a hand to her flushed cheek and twitched a pillow, but looked calm in the face of the peevish demand and stream of belligerent threats.

'Oh, it's way above my pay grade to make a decision like that, Mr Azaria.'

'Then get me someone who can make a decision—' Alekis broke off as he registered Zach's presence. 'Good, give me *your* phone, and a brandy wouldn't come amiss.'

'I must have mislaid it.' Zach's response earned him a look of approval from the flush-faced nurse.

Alekis snorted. 'It's a conspiracy!' he grumbled. 'So, what are you waiting for? Take a seat, then. Don't stand there towering over me.'

Zach did as he was bade, lowering his immaculately clad, long and lean, six-foot-five athletic frame into one of the room's easy chairs. Stretching his legs out in front of him, he crossed one ankle over the other.

'You look—'

'I look like a dying man,' came the impatient response. 'But not yet—I have things to do and so do you. I assume you do actually have your phone?'

Zach's relief at the business-as-usual attitude

was cancelled out by his concern at the shaking of the blue-veined hand extended to him.

He hid his concern beneath a layer of irony as he scrolled down the screen to find the best of the requested snapshots he'd taken several days earlier for Alekis.

'So how long before the news that I'm in here surfaces and the sharks start circling?'

Zach selected the best of the head shots he had taken and glanced up. 'Who knows?'

'Damage limitation is the order of the day, then.'

Zach nodded and extended the phone. 'I suppose if you're going to have another heart attack, you're in the right place. I'm assuming that you will tell me at some point why you sent me to a graveyard in London to stalk some woman.'

'Not stalk, take a photo…'

Zach's half-smile held irony as he responded to the correction. 'All the difference in the world. I'm curious—did it ever occur to you I'd say no?'

Zach had been due to address a prestigious international conference in London as guest speaker to an audience consisting of the cream of the financial world when Alekis had rung him with his bizarre demand, thinly disguised as a request.

Should he ever start believing his own press he could always rely on Alekis to keep his ego in check, Zach mused with wry affection as the short conversation of several days before flickered through his head.

'You want me to go *where* and do *what*?'

'You heard me. Just give the address of the church to your driver—the cemetery is opposite—then take a photo of the woman who arrives at four-thirty.'

'Try not to let it give you a heart attack this time,' Zach advised now, placing his phone into the older man's waiting hand.

'Waiting for you to deliver this picture didn't give me a heart attack. Seventy-five years of over-indulgence did, according to the doctors who tell me I should have been six feet under years ago. They also said that if I want to last even another week I should deprive myself of everything that gives life meaning.'

'I'm sure they were much more tactful.'

'I have no use for tact.'

Greedy floated into Zach's head as he watched the older man stare at the phone.

'She's beautiful, isn't she?'

Zach deemed a response unnecessary. There was no question mark over the haunting beauty of the woman captured by his phone. What he *had* questioned was not Alekis's interest, but his own fascination, bordering on obsession, with the face he couldn't stop thinking about. Until, that was, he had realised it wasn't the face, it was the puzzle of her identity, the mystery of the affair, that had tweaked his imagination, not those golden eyes.

'I'm always willing to lend a hand to a friend in need. I assume that you have lost all your fortune and no longer have access to your own personal team of private investigators in order to have needed me? How did you know she'd be there at four-thirty?'

'I have had her followed for the past two weeks.' He looked bemused that Zach would ask such an obvious question. 'And hardly a team was required… Actually I had reasons for not wanting to use in-house expertise. I was employing someone who proved to be an idiot…'

'The same person you had following her?'

'And he can whistle for his money. He was utterly inept, took any number of photographs, mostly of her back or lamp posts. And as for *covert*? She noticed him and threatened to report him for stalking… Took *his* photo, then hit him with her shopping bag. Did she see you?'

'No, I'm thinking of taking up espionage as my second career. I had no idea I was signing up for such a dangerous task. So, who is this scary lady?'

'My granddaughter.'

A quiver of surprise widened Zach's dark eyes as his ebony lashes lifted off the angle of his cheekbones. He really hadn't seen that one coming!

'Her mother was beautiful too…' The older man

seemed oblivious to Zach's reaction as he considered the photograph, his fingers shaking as he held it up. 'I think she has a look of Mia, around the mouth.' His hooded gaze lifted. 'You knew I had a daughter?'

Zach tipped his head in acknowledgement. He had of course heard the stories of the wild-child daughter. There was talk of drugs and men, but no one knew if Alekis had seen her since she'd married against his wishes, and so the story went that she'd been disinherited. This was the first time Zach had heard mention of a granddaughter, or, for that matter, heard Alekis speak of his family at all; though a portrait of his long-dead wife hung in the hallway of his palatial home on the island he owned.

'She married some loser, Parvati, threw herself away on him—to spite me, I think,' the older man brooded darkly. 'I was right. He was a useless waster, but would she listen? No, he left her when she got pregnant. All she had to do was ask and I'd have…' He shook his head, looking tired in the aftermath of emotional outburst. 'No matter, she always was as stubborn and…' His voice trailed away until he sat there, eyes half closed.

Zach began to wonder if he had fallen asleep. 'Sounds like the apple didn't fall far from the tree.'

To Zach's relief, the older man opened his eyes and directed a scowl up at Zach, which slowly faded. The smile that replaced it held a hint of pride. 'Mia was a fiery one. Like her mother to look at but...' His voice trailed away again.

If the likeness in the painting he had seen was accurate, Alekis's wife had been beautiful, though not in the same style as the granddaughter with the glowing amber eyes. Zach could see no similarity between the two. The portrait was of a beautiful woman with a beautiful face but not a face to haunt a man. Unlike the face of the woman with the golden eyes. She was Alekis's granddaughter—he was still struggling to get his head around that.

Alekis's lack of family had been something they'd had in common, part of their unlikely bond that had grown through the years. Now it turned out that there was family and he was assuming Alekis wanted to be reunited. If the older man had asked his advice, Zach would have told him it was a bad idea. But Alekis wouldn't ask or listen any more than Zach would have if someone had told him beforehand that reconnecting with his own past would leave him with memories that would offer no answers and no comfort.

'I suppose I could have made the first move. I was just waiting but she never...' He wiped a hand across his eyes and when it fell away Zach pretended not to see the moisture on the old man's cheeks.

The truth was, he was finding it uncomfortable to see the man he had always considered self-contained and unsentimental and way past being a victim of his emotions show such vulnerability. But then maybe that was what a reminder of his own mortality did to a man?

'I suppose everyone has regrets.'

'Do you?'

Zach raised his brows at the question and considered it. 'We all make mistakes,' he said, thinking of his grandmother staring out of the window with blank eyes on his last visit to the home. 'But never the same one twice.' Twice made you a fool or in love—in his eyes the latter made you the former.

He could not imagine ever allowing his heart, or at least his hormones, to rule his head. Not that he was a monk; sex was healthy and necessary but he never mixed it with sentiment, which had given him a reputation for being heartless, but he could live with that. Living with the same woman for the rest of his life? Less so!

'I regret…but it's too late for that.' Alekis's voice firmed. 'I want to make amends. I intend to leave her everything. Sorry if you thought you were getting it.'

'I don't need your money.'

'You and your damned pride! If you'd let me help you'd have got to the top a lot quicker, or at least with a lot less effort.'

'Where would be the fun in that? And you did help. You gave me an education and your advice.' Zach spoke lightly but he knew how much he owed to Alekis, and so did the shipping magnate.

'A gift beyond price, wouldn't you say?'

Zach's lips quivered into an appreciative smile. 'You really are feeling more yourself, but the moral blackmail is unnecessary, Alekis.' He spoke without heat. 'What do you want me to do?'

'Bring her to me.'

The face with the golden eyes floated into his head and Zach felt some nameless emotion flare inside him at the idea of seeing that face again.

The older man was staring again at the image on the screen.

'Will you?'

Zach's thickly defined sable brows lifted. 'Bring, as in…?' He shook his head, adding in an attempt to lighten the rather intense atmosphere that couldn't be doing Alekis's heart any good, 'I'm assuming we are not talking kidnap here.'

'It shouldn't come to that.'

'That wasn't actually an offer.'

The older man didn't appear to hear him.

'Does she have a name?' Zach asked, pretending not to see the moisture the older man wiped from the corners of his eyes.

'Katina.' Alekis's lips tightened. 'Greek only in name, she was born in England. Her history is…'

Zach was amazed to see a look close to shame wash over the older man's face.

'She has been alone for a long time. She thinks she still is. I intend to make it up to her, but I'm concerned that the shock will…'

'I'm sure she'll cope,' Zach soothed, repressing the cynical retort on the tip of his tongue. Discovering you were set to become wealthy beyond anyone's wildest dreams was the sort of shock most people recovered from quite quickly.

'It will be a culture shock. She's about to become an heiress and the target of vicious tongues and gold-diggers. She'll need to be protected…'

'From what you say she seems pretty well able to protect herself,' Zach inserted drily.

'Oh, she's clearly got spirit, but it takes more than spirit. She needs to be taught how things operate,' her grandfather continued. 'And I'm stuck in here, which is why I'm—'

Zach, who had listened with growing unease at the direction of this, cut in quickly. 'I'd love to help but that sounds pretty much like a full-time job to me.'

His mentor gave a deep sigh that made Zach's teeth clench; the smile that accompanied it was a nice blend of understanding and sadness. 'And you have every right to refuse.' Another sigh. 'You owe me nothing. Please don't run away with the idea I'm calling in a debt. I will discharge myself and—'

Zach lowered his shoulders. He knew when he was beaten.

'You know, sometimes I forget it was *me* that saved *your* life.'

The first lesson you learnt on the streets was to look after number one, the second was walk, or preferably run, away from trouble. Zach's problem was bullies. He hated them, and seeing those knife-wielding thugs surrounding the foolish old guy who was refusing to hand over his wallet had produced a red-mist moment that had led him to run towards danger and not away from it.

Zach believed nothing positive could be achieved by reflecting on the past, but if he had, his objective view would have been that there hadn't been anything remotely brave about his actions. Though stupid had flashed through his head at the first cut that had slipped between his ribs.

He might have saved the older man's life, but Alekis had given him a life and until this point asked for very little in return.

He watched, an expression of wry resignation twisting his lips, as the man's air of weary defeat melted away in a beat of his damaged heart.

The elderly Greek's smile oozed smug satisfaction. 'If you're sure?'

'Don't push it,' Zach growled out, torn between exasperation that he had been so expertly manipulated and amusement.

'It is important to control the flow of information when the news does leak. I know I can rely on you for that. The media will be all over her like a rash. We must be ready; she *must* be ready. *Go away!*'

The loud addition was directed to an unwary nurse who, to give her her due, stood her ground.

'I'll leave him to you. Good luck,' Zach added as he rose to his feet. 'You can email me the necessary,' he added before the exhausted-looking patient could react to his intention. 'Just give me her details and I'll do the rest, and in the meantime you get some rest.'

Kat danced around her small office and punched the air in triumph, before controlling the fizz of excitement still bubbling in her veins enough to retrieve the letter that she had tossed in the air after she had read it.

She read it again now, anxious that she hadn't misinterpreted it. That really *would* be awful. The tension that had slipped into her shoulders fell away as she came to the end.

It really did say what she'd thought, but what puckered her smooth brow into a slight frown was what it *didn't* say. There was a time she was expected to be there, at the address of the law firm, but no clue as to *who* was looking forward to meeting her.

She shrugged. Presumably a representative of one of the individuals or businesses known for their philanthropy to whom she had pitched her appeal—or *wasted her time with*, as some of her less optimistic-minded colleagues and volunteers had put it. Fighting against the negativity, she'd pointed out that she wasn't expecting any one person or organisation to step into the breach, but if she could persuade a handful to make some sort of donation it could mean a stay of execution for the refuge once the local authority funding was pulled the coming month.

Who knew? This could be the first of many.

There was a short tap on the door before Sue, with her nose stud, stuck her orange-streaked head around the door. 'Oh, God!' She sighed when she saw Kat's face. 'I know that look.'

'What look?'

The older woman stepped inside the room and, after closing the door, said, 'Your "campaign for a good cause" face.'

Kat blinked. 'Do I have a…?'

'Oh, you sure do, and I love—we *all* love—that you're a fighter, but there comes a time…' She sighed again, her skinny shoulders lifting before they fell. 'You've got to be a realist, love,' she told Kat earnestly. 'This place…' Her expansive gesture took in the small office with its cardboard-box system of filing—there always seemed to be something better to spend the limited resources on than office furniture. 'It's a lost cause. I've got an interview Monday. Just giving you the heads-up that I'll need the morning off.'

Kat was unable to hide her shock; her face fell. 'You're looking for another job?' If Sue, who was as upbeat as she was hard-working, had already given in... *Am I the only one who hasn't?*

'Too right I am, and I suggest you do too. There's always bills to pay and in my case mouths to feed. I care about this place too, you know, Kat.'

Kat felt a stab of contrition that her reaction might be read as judgement. 'I know that.' But the point was she didn't know what it was to be like Sue, a single parent bringing up five children and holding down two jobs.

On the brink of sharing the good news, she pulled back and moderated her response. She didn't want to raise hopes if nothing came of this.

'I know you think I'm mad, but I *really* think there's a realistic prospect someone out there cares.'

The other woman grinned. 'I know you do, and I really hope life never knocks that starry-eyed optimism out of you.'

'It hasn't so far,' Kat retorted. 'And Monday's fine. I'll cover... Good luck.'

She waited until the other woman had left before she sat down at her desk—actually, it was a table with one wobbly leg—and thought about who she might be meeting. Whoever it was didn't hang around. The meeting was scheduled for the following morning and the letter had been sent recorded delivery.

Well, she could cross the two off her list who had already sent a sympathetic but negative response, so who did that leave?

But then, did the identity of the potential donor actually matter? What mattered was that someone out there was interested enough for a meeting. So there was no beacon of light at the end of a tunnel but there was a definite flicker. Her small chin lifted in an attitude of determination. Whoever it turned out to be, she would sell her cause to them. Because the alternative was not something she wanted to contemplate—failure.

So for the rest of the day she resisted the temptation to share her news with the rest of her gloomy-looking colleagues. Not until she knew what was on offer, or maybe she just didn't want to have anyone dampen her enthusiasm with a bucket of cold-water realism? Either way there was no one to turn to for advice when she searched her wardrobe for something appropriate that evening.

There wasn't a lot to search. Her wardrobe was what designers called capsule, though maybe capsule was being generous.

It wasn't that she didn't love clothes and fashion, it was just that her budget was tight and in the past used up by impulse *bargain* buys, which inevitably sat in her wardrobe untouched and were eventually donated to a charity chop.

After a mega charity shop clear-out at the beginning of the summer and an unseasonal resolution to avoid sale racks, she had adopted a pared-down wardrobe. There had been the *one* slip. She looked at it now, hanging beside the eminently practical items. She rubbed the deep midnight-blue soft cashmere silk fabric between her fingers and gave a tiny nod; it was perfect for tomorrow's 'dress to impress'.

Smiling because her moment of weakness had been vindicated, she extracted the dress that stood out among the white shirts, T-shirts, black trousers and jeans, and hung it on the hook at the back of the bedroom door. Smoothing down the fabric, she checked it for creases, but everything about the dress managed to combine fluid draping with classic tailoring and the look screamed designer. The only fault she'd been able to find that had caused it to be downgraded to a second was the belt loop that needed a few stitches.

It had fitted so perfectly when she'd tried it on and had been marked down so much that, even though her practical head had told her there would never be an occasion in her life where the beautifully cut dress would come into it, she had bought it.

If she'd believed in fate—well, actually she did; the problem, in her experience, was not always recognising the door left ajar by fate as a golden opportunity.

It took her a little longer to dig out the heels buried among the piles in the back of the wardrobe, and she was ready. All she needed now was to go through her plan of attack. If she wanted to sell her case, make it stand out amongst the many deserving cases, she needed facts at her fingertips and a winning smile and someone with a heart to direct it at. The smile that flashed out was genuine as she caught sight of her face in the mirror... her eyes narrowed and her forehead creased in a frown of fierce determination.

So her winning smile could do with some work!

CHAPTER TWO

ZACH WAS EXPECTED. The moment he strode into the foyer his reception committee materialised. He was shown up to the empty boardroom by the senior partner—the only Asquith left in the law firm of Asquith, Lowe and Urquhart—and three underlings of the senior variety.

If Zach had thought about it—which he hadn't, because he'd had other things on his mind—he would have expected no less, considering that the amount of business Alekis sent this firm's way had to be worth enough to keep the Englishman's Caribbean tan topped up for the next millennium and then some, not to mention add a few more inches to his expanding girth.

'I will bring Miss Parvati up when she arrives. How is Mr Alekis? There have been rumours...'

Zach responded to this carefully casual addition with a fluid shrug of his broad shoulders. 'There are always rumours.'

The older man tilted his head and gave a *can't blame a man for trying* nod as he backed towards the door, an action mirrored by the three underlings, who had tagged along at a respectful distance.

Zach unfastened the button on his tailored grey jacket and, smoothing his silk tie, called after the other man before he exited the room. 'Inform me when she arrives. I'll let you know when to show her up.'

'Of course. Shall I have coffee brought in?'

His gesture took in the long table, empty but for the water and glasses at the end where Zach had pulled out a chair. Watching him, the older man found himself, hand on his ample middle, breathing in. The sharp intake of stomach-fluttering breath came with an unaccustomed pang of wistful envy that he recognised as totally irrational— you couldn't be wistful about something you had never had, and he had never had the sort of lean, hard, toned physique this man possessed. His own physical presence had a lot more to do with expensive tailoring, which permitted him to indulge his love of good food and fine wine.

'The water will be fine.' Zach reached for one of the iced bottles of designer water to illustrate the point and tipped it into a glass before he took his seat.

The door closed, and Zach glanced around

the room without much interest. The room had a gentlemen's club vibe with high ceilings and dark wooden panelled walls—not really his usual sort of environment. He had never been in a position to utilise the old-school-tie network, but he had never been intimidated by it and, more importantly, not *belonging* to this world had not ultimately hindered his progress. If he was viewed in some quarters as an outsider, it didn't keep him awake nights, and even if it had he could function pretty well on four hours' sleep.

He opened his tablet and scrolled onto the file that Alekis's office had forwarded. It was not lengthy, presumably an edited version of the full warts and all document. Zach had no problem with that; he didn't need the dirt to make a judgement. The details he did have were sufficient to give him a pretty good idea of the sort of childhood the young woman he was about to meet had had.

The fact that, like him, she had not had an easy childhood did not make him feel any *connection*, any more than he would have felt connected to someone who shared a physical characteristic with him. But he did feel it gave him an insight others might lack, the same way he knew that the innocence that had seemed to shine out from her eyes in the snapshot had been an illusion. Innocence was one of the first casualties of the sort of childhood she had had.

She had been abandoned and passed through the care system; he could see why Alekis thought he had a lot to make up for—he did. Zach was not shocked by what the mother had done—he was rarely shocked by the depths to which humans could sink—but he was mildly surprised that Alekis, who presumably had had ways of keeping tabs on his estranged daughter, had not chosen to intervene, a decision he was clearly trying to make up for now.

While many might say never too late, Zach would not. He believed there was definitely too late to undo the damage. He supposed in this instance it depended on how *much* damage had been done. What was not in question was the fact that the woman he was about to meet would know how to look after herself.

She was a survivor, he could admire that, but he was a realist. He knew you didn't survive the sort of childhood she'd had without learning how to put your own interests first, and he should know.

The indent between his dark brows deepened. It concerned him that Alekis, who would normally have been the first to realise this, seemed to be in denial. The grandfather in him was putting sentiment ahead of facts, and the fact was anyone who had experienced what this woman had was never going to fit into her grandfather's world without being a magnet for scandal.

As Zach knew, you didn't escape your past; you carried it with you and learnt to look after number one. When had *he* last put someone else's needs ahead of his own?

There was no occasion to remember.

The acknowledgement didn't cause him any qualms of conscience. You didn't get to be one of life's survivors by *not* prioritising your own interests.

And Zach was a survivor. In his book it was preferable to be considered selfish than a victim, and rather than feel bitter about his past he was in some ways grateful for it and the mental toughness it had gifted him, without which he would not have enjoyed the success he had today.

He responded to the message on his phone, his fingers flying as he texted back. He looked down at the screen of his tablet. The vividness of the woman's golden eyes, even more intense against the rest of the picture that seemed washed of colour, stared out at him before he closed it with a decisive click.

Maybe he was painting a bleaker picture. He might be pleasantly surprised—unless Alekis had deliberately hidden them, it seemed the granddaughter hadn't had any brushes with the law. Of course, that might simply mean she had stayed under the radar of the authorities, but she did seem to hold down a steady job. Perhaps the best thing the mother had ever done for her child was to abandon her.

There was the lightest of taps on the door before Asquith stepped inside the room, his hand hovering in a paternal way an inch away from the small of the back of the woman who walked in beside him.

This wasn't the fey creature from the misty graveyard, neither was it a woman prematurely hardened by life and experience.

Theos! This was possibly the most beautiful creature he had ever laid eyes on.

For a full ten seconds after she walked in, Zach's entire nervous system went into shutdown and when it flickered back into life, he had no control over the heat that scorched through his body. The sexual afterglow of the blast leaving his every nerve ending taut.

He studied her, his eyes shielded by his half-lowered eyelids and the veil of his sooty eyelashes. He felt himself resenting that it was a struggle to access even a fraction of the objectivity he took for granted as he studied her. He expected his self-control to be his for the asking, irrespective of a bloodstream with hormone levels that were off the scale.

He forced the tension from his spine, only to have it settle in his jaw, finding release in the ticcing muscle that clenched and unclenched spasmodically as he studied her. She was wearing heels, which made her almost as tall as the lawyer, who was just under six feet. She was dressed with the sort of simplicity that didn't come cheap, but to be fair the long, supple lines of her slim body would have looked just as good dressed in generic jeans and a T-shirt.

He categorised the immediate impression she projected as elegance, poise and sex...

Her attention was on the man speaking to her, so Zach had the opportunity to prolong his study of her. She stood sideways on, presenting him with her profile as she nodded gravely at something the other man was saying, eyelashes that made him think of butterfly wings fluttering against her soft, rounded, slightly flushed cheeks. It was a pretty whimsical analogy for him.

Stick to the facts, Zach, suggested the voice in his head.

He did, silently describing what he saw.

Her profile was clear cut, almost delicate. There was the suggestion of a tilt on the end of her nose, her brow high and wide. The fey creature in the snapshot had a face framed by a cloud of ebony hair; this elegant young woman's hair was drawn smoothly back into a ponytail at the nape of her neck to fall like a slither of silk between her shoulder blades almost to waist level. Dark and cloud-like in the photos, in real life it was a rich warm brown, interspersed with warm toffee streaks.

The slight tilt of her head emphasised the slender length of her swan-like dancer's neck; the same grace was echoed in her slim curves and long limbs, beautifully framed by the simplicity of the figure-skimming calf-length dress. The length of her shapely legs was further emphasised by a pair of high, spiky heels.

'I'll leave you.'

'Leave?' Kat echoed.

Zach registered the soft musicality of her voice as her feathery brows lifted in enquiry, then, the moment he had been anticipating, she turned her head. Yes, her eyes really *were* that impossible colour, a rich deep amber, the tilt at the corners creating an exotic slant and lending her beautiful face a memorable quality.

Kat had been aware of the man in the periphery of her vision, sitting at the head of the long table. Up to that point, good manners had prevented her from responding to her curiosity and looking while her escort was speaking.

She did so now, just as the figure was rising to his feet.

The first thing she had noticed about her escort was his expensive tailoring, his plummy accent and old-school tie. This man was equally perfectly tailored—minus the old-school tie. His was silk and narrow, dark against the pale of his shirt. But what he wore was irrelevant alongside the impression of raw male power that hit her with the force of a sledgehammer.

She actually swayed!

He made the massive room suddenly seem a lot smaller; in fact, she experienced a wave of claustrophobia along with a cowardly impulse to beg her escort to wait for her.

You're not a wimp, Kat, or a quitter. Appearances and first impressions, she reminded herself, were invariably misleading. She'd found the first man's air of sleek, well-tailored affluence and accent off-putting initially, and yet now, a few floors up, he appeared cosy and benevolent. In a few minutes this dark stranger might seem cosy too. Her dark-lashed gaze moved in an assessing covert sweep from his feet to the top of his sleek dark head. Or *maybe not*!

Unless you considered large sleek predators *cosy*, and there was something of the jungle cat about him, in the way he moved with the fluid grace, the restless vitality you sensed beneath the stillness that a feral creature might feel in an enclosed space.

Aware she was in danger of overreacting and allowing her imagination to run riot, she huffed out a steadying breath between her stiff lips.

'Good morning.' She gave her best businesslike smile, aiming for a blend of warm but impersonal.

Easier said than done, when there were so many conflicting emotions jostling for supremacy in her head. Not to mention the fluttery pit of her stomach. She had no idea what she had been expecting, but it hadn't been this, or him!

She never rushed to judgement. She prided herself on her ability not to judge by appearances, so the rush of antagonism she had felt the moment his dark eyes had locked on hers was bewildering—and it hadn't gone away.

Her heart was racing, and it wasn't the only thing that had sped up. Everything had, including her perceptions, which were heightened to an extraordinary, almost painful degree, though they were focused less on the room with its background scent of leather and wood and more on the man who dominated with such effortless ease.

She had taken in everything about him in that first stunned ten seconds. The man stood several inches over six feet, and inside the elegant suit his build was lean yet athletic, with broad shoulders that were balanced perfectly by long, long legs. The strong column of his neck was the same deep shade of gold as his face, the warm and vibrant colour of his skin emphasised by the contrasting paleness of his shirt.

He was sinfully good-looking, if your taste ran to perfect. Such uncompromising masculinity attached to perfect symmetry, hard angles and carved planes, a wide mouth that was disturbingly sensual and the dark-as-night eyes framed by incredible jet lashes set under dark, strongly delineated brows.

There was no reaction to the smile she somehow kept pasted in place. She told herself to keep it together as she struggled to make the mental adjustments required.

'Oh, God!' It wasn't the pain in her knee when she hit the chair leg that made her cry out, it was the sight of the carefully arranged contents of the folder she carried sliding to the floor. 'Sorry,' she muttered as she bent to pick up the scattered papers, jamming them haphazardly into the folder.

Walk, think and string two syllables together, Kat. It's not exactly multitasking! It's all on your phone so it's not a disaster!

Cheeks hot, she straightened up. Forget old-school tie, *this* was who she was dealing with. *Fine.* Except, of course, it *wasn't* fine; she *was* making an impression, but not the intended one. Having gathered the papers, she promptly dropped them again. She bit her tongue literally to stop herself blurting a very unladylike curse.

Zach watched her silky hair fall over one shoulder as she fumbled for the scattered papers. The action drew attention to the curve of her behind, and as the soft, silky dark material of her dress stretched tight so did his nerve endings.

He could not recall the last time he had needed to fight his way through a fog of blind lust. If Alekis had had a window into his mind at that moment he might have doubted casting him in the role of protector and mentor. Or maybe not. There was some sense in it. Who better to guard the fluffy chick than a fox? Always supposing the fox in question could keep his own baser instincts in check.

Not that this creature was fluffy, she was more silky-smooth. *Smooth all over?*

Calming down this illicit line of distracting speculation, he let the silence stretch. It was amazing how many people felt the need to fill a silence, saying things that revealed more than a myriad searching questions.

Unfortunately, and uncomfortably on this occasion, in a moment of role reversal his own mind felt the need to fill the silence.

Alekis trusted him. The question was, did he trust himself?

The moment of self-doubt passed; even taking the trust issue with Alekis out of the equation, the logic of keeping the personal and professional separate remained inescapable.

'Won't you take a seat?'

She responded to the offer with relief; her knees

were literally shaking. 'Thank you.' At least the table between them meant she was not obliged to offer her hand. Instead, she tipped her head and smiled. 'I'm Kat.'

'Take a seat, Katina.' He watched the surprise flare in her amazing eyes and slide into wariness before she brought her lashes down enough to veil her expression momentarily.

The use of her *full* name, which no one ever used, threw her slightly. Well, actually, more than slightly.

He couldn't know it, but the last person to call her that had been her mother.

For many years Kat had believed that while she could hear her mother's voice in her head, her mother was not gone…she was coming back. Nowadays the childhood conviction was gone and so was her mother's voice. The memory might be lost but she did know that her name on her mother's lips had not sounded anything like it did when this man rolled his tongue around the syllables.

'Th-thank you,' she stuttered. Recovering from the shaky moment, she gathered her poise around herself, protective-blanket style. 'Just Kat is fine,' she added finally, taking the seat he had gestured towards and reflecting that it wasn't at all fine.

Though she was normally all for informality, she would have been much happier with a formal, distant *Miss*…or *Ms* or maybe even, *hey, you*. It wasn't just her physical distance she felt the need to keep from this man. His dark gaze seemed able to penetrate her very soul.

She forced herself to forget his disturbing mouth, equally disturbing eyes, the almost explosive quality he projected, and move past the weird inexplicable antagonism. She was here to make a pitch, and save the precious resource that the community was in danger of losing. This was not about her—she just had to stay focused on the prize.

All great advice in theory, but in reality, with those eyes drilling into her like lasers... Were lasers cold? She pushed away the thought and tried to dampen the stream of random thoughts that kept popping into her head down to a slow trickle.

Reminding herself that a lot of people were relying on her helped; the fact she was distracted by the muscle that was clenching and unclenching in his lean cheek did not.

'Water?'

Repressing the impulse to ask him if he had anything stronger, she shook her head.

'I'm fine,' she said, thinking, *If only!*

Nervous was actually how she was feeling and this man was probably wondering why the hell she was here.

She cleared her throat. 'I'm sure you have a lot of questions?'

His dark brows lifted; there was nothing feigned

about his surprised reaction. 'I would have thought *you'd* have a lot of questions.'

True, she did. She gave voice to the first one that popped into her head. 'What do I call you?'

It wasn't really a change of expression, but his heavy eyelids flickered and left her with the distinct impression this wasn't the sort of question he had anticipated. She took a deep breath and tried again.

'It really doesn't matter to us *who* you represent—when I say it doesn't matter I don't mean... We would never accept anything from a...an...illegitimate source—obviously.'

'Obviously,' Zach said, realising for the first time that she wasn't wondering why she was there, because she thought she knew.

He was intrigued.

His eyes slid to her plump lips. Intrigued had a much better ring to it than fascinated.

'Not that you look like a criminal or anything,' she hastened to assure him.

His lips twitched. 'Would you like to see character references...?'

She chose to ignore the sarcasm while observing that even when his mouth smiled his eyes remained as expressionless and hard as black glass. There was no warmth there at all. She found herself wondering what warmed that chill, and then gathered her wandering thoughts back to the moment and her reason for being here, which wasn't thinking about his eyes, or, for that matter, any other part of his dauntingly perfect body.

'We are just grateful that you are willing to consider contributing.'

'*We?*'

She flushed and refused to be put off by his sardonic tone. 'This *we*...' Kat pulled the folder from her bag and pointed to the logo on the cover. 'The Hinsdale project and family refuge. *Dame* Laura...' she put a gentle emphasis on the title; it was hard to tell sometimes but some people were impressed by such things, not that she had to pretend pride or enthusiasm as she told him '...began it back in the sixties when there was just the one house, a mid-terrace, a two-up two-down. It was all a bit basic.'

'And now?'

'We have extended into the houses both sides, the entire row, and can take thirty-five women at any one time, depending, obviously, on the number of children. In the eighties the chapel across the road came up for sale and we bought it. Now it houses the nursery and crèche, which is available for women when they have moved out. It also contains a drop-in centre, which provides legal help and so forth. Dame Laura was personally involved, right up to her death.'

Had her own mother found Hinsdale, or a similar place, both their lives might have been very different.

Zach watched the wave of sadness flicker across her expressive face. Letting this interview play out a little longer might be on shaky ground morally, but practically it would provide a swifter insight into this woman whom he was meant to be *babysitting*.

'And what is your role?' Zach was experiencing a strange reluctance to abandon his mental image of a person so damaged they never looked at anything other than their own self-interest—a person, in short, much like himself.

The frown that came with the unbidden flicker of self-awareness faded as he watched her beautiful face light up with a glow of conviction and resolution as she leaned forward in her seat, losing the nervousness as she answered proudly.

'I run the refuge, along with a great team, many of whom are volunteers, as was I initially. I began by volunteering at the crèche when I was at school, and after I left I was offered a salaried position. I like to think Dame Laura would have been proud of what we have achieved.' Kat had met the redoubtable lady once; she had been frail but as sharp as a tack and totally inspirational. 'Her legacy lives on.' Embarrassed, Kat swallowed the emotional lump in her throat and reminded herself that there was a fine line between enthusiasm and looking a little unhinged. 'We have a dedicated staff and, as I said, so many volunteers. We are part of the community and don't turn anyone away.'

'That must make forward planning difficult.'

'We build in flexibility—'

He felt a twinge of admiration that, despite the starry-eyed enthusiasm, she was not so naive that she didn't know how to sidestep a difficult answer.

'Is that possible fiscally?'

'Obviously in the present financial climate—'

'How much do you need?'

The hard note of cold cynicism in his interruption made her blink, then rush to reassure. 'Oh, please, don't think for one moment we are expecting you to cover the total shortfall.'

'As negotiating tactics go, that, *Kat*...' the way he drawled her name made the fine hairs on the nape of her neck stand on end '...was not good—it was bad. It was abysmal.'

Her expression stiffened and grew defensive. 'I came here under the impression that you *wanted* to contribute to the refuge.' She struggled to contain the antagonism that sparkled in her eyes as she planted her hands on the table and leaned in. 'Look, if this is about me... There are other people who could do my job. The important thing is the work.'

'Do you think everything is about you?'

Kat felt her face flush. 'Of course not, it just felt...feels as if you find me...'

'So you are saying you'd sacrifice yourself to save this place?'

She swallowed, wondering if that was what it was going to take. Obviously it was a price she would be willing to pay, but only as a last resort. *Crawl and grovel if that's what he wants, Kat.* She heaved a deep sigh and managed an *almost* smile.

'You don't like me, fine.' *Because I really don't like you.*

Zach watched the internal struggle reflected on her face. This was a woman who should never play poker. As a born risk-taker, he enjoyed that form of relaxation.

She left a space for him to deny the claim.

He didn't.

'But, please,' she begged, 'don't allow that to influence your decision. I am one person easy to replace, but there is a dedicated staff who work incredibly hard.' Breathing hard, she waited for a response, the slightest hint of softening, but there was none.

Her chin went up; she was in nothing-to-lose territory.

She flicked to the first page of the thin folder, except the first page was now somewhere in the middle so it took her a few moments to locate it. 'I have the facts and figures; the average stay of a client is…' With a sigh she turned the page of figures over. It wasn't the right one. 'The average doesn't matter. Everyone who comes is different and we try to cater to their individual needs. The woman who is my deputy first arrived as a client. She was in an abusive relationship…'

A nerve along his jaw quivered. 'Her partner hit her?'

The hairs on the nape of her neck lifted in response to the danger in his deceptively soft question. Underneath the beautiful tailoring she sensed something dangerous, almost feral, about this man. A shiver traced a sticky path up her spine as she struggled to break contact with his dark eyes.

'No, he didn't.' He hadn't needed to. He had isolated Sue from her family and friends and had controlled every aspect of her life before she'd finally left. Even her thoughts had not been her own. 'It's not always about violence. Sometimes the abuse is emotional,' she said quietly. 'But she now works for us full-time, is a fantastic mum and was voted onto the local council. The refuge has helped so many and it will again in future, the cash-flow situation is—'

Her own earnest flow was stemmed by his upheld hand. 'I am sure your cause is very worthy, but that is not why you were invited here.'

'I don't understand…'

'I had never heard of your refuge, or your Dame Laura.'

As his words sank in, the throb of anger in her head got louder; her voice became correspondingly softer. 'Then why the hell am I here?'

It was an indulgence, but he took a moment to enjoy the flashing amber eyes that viewed him with utter contempt.

'I am here to represent Alekis Azaria.'

The name seemed vaguely familiar to Kat but she had no idea why. She leaned forward, arching a questioning brow. *Greek...?*

He nodded. He had seen several reactions to Alekis's name before, ranging from awe to fear, but hers was a first. She clearly didn't have a clue who he was.

'Like you.'

She frowned, then realised his mistake. 'Oh, not really. The name, you mean? Oh, I suppose I must have some Greek blood, but I've never been there. Are you...?' she asked, searching for some sort of explanation, some sort of connection to explain him and this interview.

'I am Greek, like Alekis.'

'So why did this man who I have never heard of invite me here?' The entire thing made no sense to her. 'Who is he?'

CHAPTER THREE

'HE'S YOUR GRANDFATHER.'

He watched as the bemused confusion drawn on her face froze and congealed. As her wide eyes flickered wide in shock.

It took a conscious effort for Zach to hold on to his objectivity as she gasped like a drowning person searching for air. She sucked in a succession of deep breaths.

'I have no family.' Her voice was flat, her expression empty of the animation that had previously lit it. 'I have no one, so I can't have a grandfather.'

He pushed away an intrusive sliver of compassion and the squeeze of his heart and hardened his voice as he fell back on facts, always more reliable than sentiment.

'We all have two grandfathers, even me.'

Another time she might have questioned the significance of the *even me* but Kat was in shock. The sheer unexpectedness of what he had said had felt like walking…no, *running* full pelt into a brick wall that had suddenly appeared in the middle of a flower-filled meadow.

'I don't even know who my *father* is, other than a name on a birth certificate.' It had never crossed her mind to track down the man who had abandoned her pregnant mother. The decision to search for her mother had not been one she had taken lightly, though, as it turned out, she had already been five years too late. 'Why should I want any contact with his family?'

Zach narrowed his eyes, recalling the one line in the file on the man Alekis's daughter had married in defiance of her father's wishes. 'He might have a family, but I don't have that information.'

'I don't understand…'

'It is your mother's family, or rather her father, that I am representing.'

She listened to his cold, dispassionate explanation before sitting there in silence for several moments, allowing her disjointed thoughts to coalesce.

'She had a family…' She faltered, remembering bedtime stories, the tall tales of a sun-drenched childhood. Was even a *tiny* part of that fantasy based on reality? The thought made her ache for her mother, far away from home and rejected.

'Your grandfather is reaching out to you.'

Shaking her head, Kat rose to her feet, then

subsided abruptly as her shaking legs felt too in-substantial to support her.

'Reaching…' She shook her head and the slither of silk down her back rippled, making Zach wonder what it would look like loose and spread against her pale gold skin. 'I don't want *anyone* reaching out to me.' Her angry amber eyes came to rest accusingly on his handsome face. She knew there was a reason she had never trusted too-good-looking men besides prejudice and the fact the man who had spiked her drink all those years ago had been the one all the girls in the nightclub had been drooling over. 'Is this some sort of joke?'

'It is real.' As real as the colour of those pain-filled, angry, magnificent eyes.

'He's rich?'

Her words did make it sound as though a yes would be a good thing. This was not avarice speaking, he realised, but anger. The former would have made his life a lot easier.

'He is not poor.'

Her trembling lips clamped tight, the pressure blanching the colour from her skin as she fought visibly for composure.

'My mum was… She was poor, you see…*very* poor.' She eyed him with contempt, not even bothering to attempt to describe the abject hand-to-mouth existence that had driven her mother to drugs and the men who supplied them. A man who looked like him, dressed like him and oozed the confidence that came from success and affluence could not even begin to understand that life and the events that trapped people in the living hell of degradation.

'Yes.'

One of the reasons she rarely mentioned her early years was the way people reacted. She mentally filed them into two camps: the ones that looked at her with pity and those that felt uneasy and embarrassed.

His monosyllabic response held none of the above, just a statement of fact. Ironic, really, that a response she would normally have welcomed only added another layer to the antagonism that swirled inside her head as she looked at him. By the second he was becoming the personification of everything she disliked most in a person. Someone born to privilege and power without any seeming moral compass.

Ignoring the voice in her head that told her she was guilty of making the exact sort of rush or, in this case, more a *stampede* to judgement that she'd be the first to condemn, she sucked in a deep sustaining breath through flared nostrils.

Despite her best efforts, her voice quivered with emotion that this man would *definitely* see as a weakness. '*He* didn't reach out to her…'

'No.'

Her even white teeth clenched. 'Where was *he* when his daughter needed him? If he makes the same sort of grandfather as he made father, why would I want to know him?'

'I don't know...' He arched a satiric brow and pretended to consider the answer. 'He's rich?'

Her chin lifted to the defiant angle he was getting very familiar with. It was a long time since Zach had been regarded with such open contempt. *Better than indifference!*

The knee-jerk reaction of his inner voice brought a brief frown to his brow before he turned his critical attention to the play of expression across her flawless features. He had never encountered anyone who broadcast every thought in their heads quite so obviously before.

The concept of a professional guard would be alien to her. Though in her defence, this *wasn't* professional to her—it was very personal. He was getting the idea that everything with this woman might be.

For someone who compartmentalised every aspect of his life, the emotional blurring was something that appalled him.

'So you're of the "everyone has a price" school of thought,' she sneered.

'They do.'

His man-of-few-words act was really starting to get under her skin.

'I don't. I'm not interested in money and… and…*things*!'

He arched a satiric brow. 'That might be a more impressive statement if you hadn't come here with a begging bowl.'

She fought off the angry flush she could feel rising up her neck. 'That is *not* the same.'

He dragged his eyes up from the blue-veined pulse that was beating like a trapped wild bird at the base of her slender throat. This might be the moment he told himself to remember that the un-touched, fragile look had never been a draw for him. He had no protective instincts to arouse.

'If you say so.'

His sceptical drawl was an insult in itself.

'I am *not* begging. This isn't for me.'

He cut her off with a bored, 'I know, it is for the greater good. So consider that for the moment— consider how much you could help the *greater good* if you had access to the sort of funds that your grandfather has.'

He allowed himself the indulgence of watching the expressions flicker across her face for several seconds before speaking.

'You see, everyone *does* have a price—even you.'

'There is no *even me*. And I'm not suggesting I'm a better person than anyone else!' she fired back.

Zach watched her bite her lip before lifting her

chin and found himself regretting his taunt. As exasperating as her attitude was, she had just received news that was the verbal equivalent of a gut punch.

And she had come out fighting.

'If you say so.'

She blinked hard, not prepared to let it go. 'I *do* say so, and,' she choked out, 'I really don't want to know the sort of person who would abandon his daughter.'

'Maybe she abandoned him?'

The suggestion drew a ferocious glare. On one level he registered how magnificent she looked furious, on another he realised that he was now in uncharted territory—he was playing it by ear. Zach trusted his instincts; his confidence was justified but, in this instance, it had turned out to be massively misplaced.

The unorthodox role assigned to him had been unwelcome, but he had approached it as he would anything. He'd thought that he had factored in all the possibilities…had considered every reaction and how to counter them to bring about the desired outcome with the least effort on his part.

Pity she didn't read the same script, Zach!

In his own defence, it hadn't seemed unreasonable to assume that the idea of being wealthy beyond any person's wildest dreams would swiftly negate any anger the heiress might feel towards the absentee grandparent.

He had never found it particularly admirable when people were willing to disadvantage themselves for a point of principle. He found it even less so now, when those so-called principles were making his own life hard work.

Not that it crossed his mind that in the long run she would reject the fortune. She'd find a way to trick herself eventually into believing she wasn't betraying her principles. He just had to help her get to that point a little quicker.

'He was the parent,' she quivered out. 'Parents care for their children.'

'In a perfect world, yes.' But, as she of all people should well know, the world was not perfect. It took a very stubborn idealist to retain a belief system like hers in light of her personal experiences.

She gritted her teeth. 'It's got nothing to do with a perfect world. It's called unconditional love. Not that I'd expect someone like you to know anything about that.'

'You'd be right, I don't,' he lied, pushing away the image that had materialised without warning in his head. His mother's thin, tired face, her work-worn hands. The memory was irrevocably linked with pain, which was why he didn't think about it, *ever*. 'Do you?'

The sudden attack threw her on the defensive. 'I

see women willing to lay down their lives for their children every day of my working life.'

'Does that make up for your own mother abandoning you?'

He ignored the kick to his conscience when she flinched as though he had struck her. The illusion of fragility vanished as her chin lifted and she looked at him with angry eyes.

'None of this is about my mother.'

'Are you trying to tell me you're not angry with her for dumping you? My mother left me because she died...and for a long time I hated her for it.' They were words he'd never even thought, let alone voiced before, and they came with a massive slug of guilt and anger that her attitude had dredged up memories he had consigned to history. 'And you expect me to believe that you were never angry that you got dumped on a doorstep somewhere?' Maybe she genuinely didn't remember and that was why she was able to continue to lie to herself.

'It was a car park of a doctor's surgery. She knew that someone would help me, that I'd be safe.'

Safe... He closed his eyes, trying to banish the poignant image in his head of a dark-haired child standing there waiting for a mother who never came back.

'Some people should not have children,' Zach

condemned. He had decided long ago that he was one of them. It was too easy for a bad parent to scar their children, so why take the risk?

'She needed help, she had nowhere to go—'

'I find your determination to see this woman as some innocent victim slightly perverse. She was the one who walked away from your grandfather. And she was an adult, not a child.'

Unable to argue with the facts the way he presented them, she snapped back. 'If this so-called grandfather of mine is so anxious to make contact, why isn't he here? Why send you?'

'He's in intensive care.'

It was a slight exaggeration; according to his latest update, Alekis had been downgraded from high dependency to whatever the medical equivalent was. He was the next step up...the walking wounded, maybe?

Her reaction was everything he had expected from someone who seemed to have *bleeding heart* stamped into her DNA. Like a pricked balloon, her anger deflated with an almost audible hiss.

Her eyes slid from his. 'Well, I'm sorry about that,' she mumbled stiffly. 'But I have no room in my life for someone I despise—' She broke off as he suddenly leaned back in his leather seat and laughed.

'That's it, of course!'

'What's *it*?'

'It's just I've been wondering who you remind me of.'

The suspicion in her eyes deepened. 'What are you talking about?'

'Someone who doesn't understand the word *compromise*, who can't forgive anyone who lets them down—in fact, anyone, even family, no, es-*pecially* family, who doesn't live up to their idea of what is right...' He arched a dark brow. 'Sounding familiar?'

It took her a few seconds to divine his meaning. Her horrified reaction was instantaneous. 'I am *nothing* like my grandfather.'

'Well, that's an improvement. You admit you have one now. I've never put much faith in the whole gene thing. I might have to rethink it—you've never met the man and yet in your own way you are as stubborn and self-righteous as Alekis.'

'How dare you?'

'Easily.' He dismissed her outrage with a click of his long fingers. 'Your grandfather couldn't forgive your mother so he lost her. You can't forgive him and you're willing to reject him when he makes the first move.'

'A move that was twenty-four years coming!'

'Granted.'

Kat's head had sunk forward, her chin almost on her chest, so that her expression was hidden from him as she muttered, 'I'm nothing like him.'

'Prove it.'

She lifted her head in response to the soft challenge, making herself look at him, mainly because once their eyes were connected it was difficult to break that connection, she observed angrily.

'You are a very manipulative man.'

He gave what she considered a heartless laugh, which sadly didn't make it any the less attractive.

'I'm impressed. It takes most people much longer to figure that one out.'

'And by then it's too late,' she said bitterly as she realised it already was for her. Like it or not, she had been put in a position where she had to prove that the future of the refuge was more important than…what? She realised that it hadn't been spelt out yet what her side of any bargain would be.

'What does he expect from me?'

'Alekis?' His broad shoulders lifted in a negligent shrug. 'You should ask him that.'

She squeezed her eyes closed, then opened them wide. 'Do I have any other family?' The sudden possibility that she had an entire family out there, aunts, uncles, cousins, felt strange…and yet exciting.

'Not that I am aware of,' he said, feeling quite irrationally guilty when the spark faded from her eyes. Another emotion broke through his defences that Zach couldn't put a name to, didn't even try. It took seconds for him to douse it, but the memory of that nameless feeling remained like a discordant echo as he responded to the question with evasion that came easily.

'But again, I suggest you should ask the man himself. I am not privy to all his secrets.'

She nodded. 'And if I do…see him…how does that work?'

Before he could congratulate himself on a job well done she gave a fractured little sigh and added, 'Does he have any *idea* what sort of life she led? The places, the men…?'

Without warning an image of the little girl she had once been flashed into his head again, along with a compulsion to ask, 'Do you remember?'

'She used to tell me stories.' Without warning her eyes filled with tears; the stories were true. 'Does he live on an island?' she asked, remembering the wistful quality in her mother's voice when she told those stories. 'He didn't want us and now I—I don't have a grandfather. I don't have anybody.'

He clenched his jaw as the plaintive cry from the heart threatened the professional distance he needed to retain. 'I know this has been a shock.'

She gave a bitter little laugh. *'You think?'*

Shock? Was that what you called making someone question everything she'd thought she knew about her life?

'Look, I have no vested interest in this. I am

simply the messenger boy. You make your decision and I'll relay it.'

She took a deep sustaining breath and looked him straight in the eye. 'I'll do it.' *Oh, God, what am I doing?* 'So, what happens now? If I agree to see him, I'm assuming he can't come here…unless that was a lie?'

'He is ill.'

'So that is real?'

He actually took some comfort from the fact that she was not *quite* as naive as she appeared, though even if she turned out to be half as naive it would be cause for serious concern.

'I wasn't lying. Alekis is seriously ill.'

'Is he in pain?'

'Not that I know of. Do you want him to be?'

Her eyes flew wide in comic-book shock-horror fashion. 'What sort of person do you think I am?' *'I think you're—'*

The driven quality in his unfinished words made her shake her head in puzzled confusion.

'You want to know what happens next?'

Diverted, she nodded.

'The plan is for me to take you to Tackyntha via Athens, where you will meet your grandfather before his next surgery.' The doctors had agreed with the utmost reluctance to Alekis's plan to meet them at the airport, and then only after he had agreed to have a full medical team with him.

She shook her head. 'Tackyntha?'

'It is your grandfather's home, an island.'

'Where my mother lived.'

'I presume so.'

'So, you want me to go to the hospital.'

The obvious solution, but Alekis was determined that when he met his granddaughter he would not be lying in a hospital bed. 'At the airport.'

'And what if I say no?'

'I'd say fair enough, though it's a shame because your cause sounded pretty deserving.'

'Do you work for him?'

His lips twitched. 'He did offer, but, no, I do not work for Alekis.'

'Does he think you can buy love? Buy me?' Her words had an angry, forlorn sound.

'That is not in my field of expertise.'

'What *is* your area of expertise?'

'Well, it's *not* babysitting reluctant heiresses.'

She responded to the barely concealed disdain in his observation with an equally snooty glare of her own. 'I do not require a babysitter, thank you.'

'Let me rephrase it. You need to learn the rules of the society you're about to enter.'

She pounced angrily on the refined definition. 'So that I don't embarrass my grandfather, you mean! Oh, to hell with this. My home is here. I'm needed here.'

'Really? You already told me that you are not irreplaceable. That you have a talented second-in-command whose task, I think, would be a lot easier if your refuge had financial security. Besides, being an heiress does not make you rich in the present, but you will be a target for shady gold-diggers and tabloid journalists, which is where I come in.'

'So, what are you—a bodyguard or a babysitter?'

'I am a man at the end of his patience,' he intoned grimly. 'Look, the options are you flounce off or give me the details so that I can arrange a bank transfer into your refuge's accounts.'

'And what do I have to do?'

'Come and say hello to a dying old man.' For starters, he added silently, before reminding himself that her future and her happiness were not his business.

Who said be careful what you wished for? Maybe, she reflected grimly, someone who had dreamt of finding a family only to have it feel… How *did* she feel?

Unravelling the confused tangle of emotions she was struggling with, Kat knew that a dream come true wasn't meant to feel this way. 'So, who would he have left his money to if he hadn't decided to make up for a quarter of a century and look for me?'

'Me, I would imagine. However, you can relax. I don't need it.'

Which explained the arrogant manner and the air of self-importance.

'If I do come with you to Greece, I will need some guarantees. Firstly, I need to know that the future of the refuge is guaranteed.'

'My word is not enough for you?'

Her eyes narrowed at the hauteur in his manner. 'In writing, for my lawyer to check over.' Her expression dared him to challenge the fact she had a lawyer. Well, Mike *was* a lawyer, though not hers, but lawyer sounded so much more impressive and businesslike than her friend from her baking class who'd like to be more.

'Agreed,' he said calmly. 'You can have the papers by the end of the day.'

'And I need to know that I can leave whenever I like.'

The idea that he or Alekis had any control over her movements was something he allowed to pass. 'Two months.'

'What?'

'You will give your grandfather two months to get to know you. That only seems fair, wouldn't you say?'

Nothing about this seemed *fair* to Kat, who nodded. 'Two months.' She started to get to her feet and stopped. 'I don't know your name.'

'Enter the name Zach Gavros into your search engine and you'll find out all you need to know about me. Some of it might even be true.'

CHAPTER FOUR

SOMEONE FILLED KAT'S glass with the wine from the party-sized box that she was pretty sure Zach Gavros would have turned his autocratic nose up at. It was still in her hand as she slipped out of the room, where the mood was definitely party, and into the relative quiet of the office. Though no longer *her* office.

She had said goodbye to everyone earlier, fighting the emotional lump in her throat, reminding herself that she was the only one, barring Sue, who knew that this was a permanent parting. The goodbye was of the 'for ever' variety.

Maybe she would come back after two months, but it didn't seem fair for her to ask Sue to step down when or if she returned, so she was making a clean break. Which had left her with no real option but to tell Sue, considering she was relying on her deputy to step into her shoes, the task that wasn't as easy as she had hoped. While she had been convincing a sceptical Sue how perfect she was for the job and how smooth the transition would be, Kat realised just how true it was. She supposed everyone liked to think they were indispensable, that they would leave a hole, be missed, but it was depressing to realise that she was so easy to replace.

'You should go back to the party,' she said to Sue, who she had seen slip away a few minutes earlier. The older woman, who was bent over a carboard box of files, straightened up and nodded.

'I will, but I couldn't let you go without a last hug.'

Feeling the tears press against her eyelids, Kat blinked and turned her head, putting her half-full glass down next to a pile of books on a cabinet. 'Nice photos,' she said, her glance taking in the framed photos of her children that Sue had already arranged on what was now *her* desk.

Sue looked anxious. 'I hope you don't mind?'

'Of course not,' Kat responded, feeling guilty because she had minded—just a bit.

'So, when do you want me to tell the others that you're not coming back from the *management course*?' Sue asked, framing the words with inverted commas. She had made no secret that she was mystified by Kat's determination to keep the truth under wraps, and Kat hadn't really known how to explain it herself. It was hard to tell other people about something that still seemed unreal to her. Besides, they might look at her the way Sue had initially, as though she'd changed or she were a different person.

Well, she wasn't, and she didn't intend to be. Kat was determined that, whatever happened, she would hang on to her own identity. If her grandfather or Zach Gavros thought they could mould her into something she wasn't, they would soon learn otherwise.

Of course, she had searched for his name. There was plenty of information there to give her an insight into the man her grandfather had chosen to tutor her in how the super-rich behaved, and also a few significant gaps.

His past seemed something of a mystery, which had sparked a thousand conspiracy theories. A favourite being that he had underworld connections. Another that he was Alekis's bastard son, which would make him her... No, that *couldn't* be right, she decided, sure that there could be no blood connection between them.

There were almost as many stories of his financial genius and ruthless dedication to amassing wealth as there were to the sleek cars he drove, and the even sleeker women who lined up to have their hearts broken by him.

And to be fair, in a number of cases their public profiles and careers had been enhanced by their association with the man. Kat didn't feel it was fair, though, as an image floated into her head of her mother's grave as it had been when she'd finally found it. Overgrown, untended…lonely. Her mother's heart had not been as resilient as the women whose names had been associated with Zach Gavros, but she liked to think that her mother had finally found a man worthy of her love. The beautiful gravestone in the cemetery gave her hope.

Kat pushed away the intruding thoughts with a firm little shake of her head. She smiled at Sue.

'That's up to you. You're the boss.' A sudden whoop from the other room, where the party was still in full swing, made her turn her head. When she looked back, Sue was looking at her suitcase.

'That is one very small case for a new life.'

'Just what I was thinking.'

Both women turned to the owner of the pleasant voice—*pleasant* was a good description of the man who was standing in the doorway. A little above average height, he was fairish and good-looking. Mike's newly acquired and carefully tended beard made him look less boyish and gave him, according to him, the maturity his clients expected of a solicitor earmarked for partner in a successful practice.

'I did knock but nobody heard. Am I too early?'

'Perfect timing, and I always travel light,' Kat told them both truthfully, seeing no need to explain that it was a hangover from her childhood, when for years she had been utterly certain that the mother who had left her sitting on the car-park wall of a health centre would come back to her. Her faith had been absolute; she had kept her small suitcase stowed neatly under her bed, packed, ready for the day her mum would come to claim her. Which was probably why none of the early foster placements had ever stuck, and the couple who had been interested in adopting her had backed out. *Polite,* she'd heard them tell her case worker, but unable to respond to love. They hadn't understood that Kat didn't need a family, she already had one, though seeing as they had said she was a polite child she hadn't wanted to upset them by explaining this.

In the end she'd found her way into a long-term foster home. A mad, hectic household with a rare and marvellous couple who didn't expect love, they just gave it, and they never mentioned her case under the bed.

Kat still had a packed case under her bed that she didn't have to explain, because Kat didn't share her bed or her history with anyone.

'You know everyone is going to be gutted they didn't get to say goodbye properly.'

Kat smiled. For a day or two, a week maybe, they might miss her. Might even say some affectionate *remember when* things about her in the future, but people forgot and that, she reminded herself before she slipped into a self-pitying spiral, was the way it should be. She would be in a position now to help them more from a distance than she ever could have here.

'What shall I tell them when you don't come back?'

'That's up to you. Like I keep saying, you'll be the boss, you'll do things your way. Oh, sorry!' She straightened the photo her elbow had nudged. 'This one of Sara is so cute. She looks just like you.'

'So everyone keeps telling me.'

Kat placed it carefully back down. The photo was the reason why Sue would always be missed, never forgotten. She had family. Shrugging off the wave of sadness tinged with envy that threatened to envelop her, Kat picked up her case and reminded herself that she travelled light, something that Sue, with all her responsibilities, couldn't do. She was lucky.

'This is your office—you might even splurge on that new desk I never got around to getting. Nobody suspects, do they?' She nodded towards the door, behind which there was the gentle hum of laughter.

'Not a thing.'

'I must be a much better liar than I thought.'

No one had had any problem accepting that a

philanthropist who wanted to remain nameless had appeared, and that he was willing to not only fund the shortfall, but very generously fund the expansion of an annex and playground they had always dreamt of, and send Kat on a management course. And why shouldn't they? Everyone loved a happy ending.

Sue's reaction to the full story had made her realise that in most people's eyes she had her own happy ending. She was an heiress; she was living the dream. The dream of so many children living in care.

Not hers. Maybe she just didn't dream big. She had never thought of castles…just somewhere small, enough money to pay the bills and a mum. Her little fantasies had never contained any male figures; her own father, she knew, had walked out before she was born, and the men in her mother's life afterwards, well, the moments of peace she remembered coincided with their absences.

The only male figure who had been a reassuring presence in her life had been her foster father, but when he had died completely unexpectedly she had seen first-hand how devastated his wife, Nell, had been.

So the options, it seemed to Kat, were between being involved with a man who turned out to a bastard who abused or deserted you, or a man who, to quote dear Nell, you 'loved so much you became half a person after you lost them'. Those heartbroken words had stayed with Kat, as had the haunted, empty look in her foster mum's eyes.

Neither of the above seemed an option anyone with half a brain would voluntarily choose, though maybe falling in love removed the choice?

She was open-minded about the power of love, but it was a power she had never felt and she didn't feel deprived. Actually, she'd started to wonder, if you *had* to have a relationship—and the world did seem to be constructed for pairs—a relationship without love might be the way to go?

A choice made for common-sense reasons with someone you knew was nice and dependable— like Mike?

It was ironic that lately she'd even been contemplating saying yes, the next time he asked her out. Though that wasn't going to happen now.

Mike picked up her case. 'You sure about this?' he asked, his expression concerned.

'Of course she is—it's like a fairy tale and she's the princess. Aren't you excited? Your life is going to change.'

Fighting the impulse to yell, *I liked my old life,* she lifted her shoulders in a delicate shrug, smiling to take the edge off her words.

'I quite liked the old one. I'm still a bit in shock,' she added, feeling she had to defend her lack of enthusiasm as she returned Sue's hug and gave a sniff. 'Stop that,' she begged the weeping Sue. 'I said I was not going to cry.'

She did, a little, and Mike, being tactful, didn't comment on her sniffles as they drove along. Instead, he kept up a desultory anecdotal conversation that required nothing from her but the occasional nod and smile until they reached the private airfield.

A barrier lifted as they approached, and they were waved through to a parking area that appeared empty apart from two limousines parked at the far end.

Mike lifted her case from the boot and turned to where she stood waiting, her slender shoulders hunched against a chill autumnal breeze. 'I've done some research, and your grandfather, Kat, he's mega wealthy.'

Kat nodded. She too had looked up her grandfather's name and seen the results that spilled out. Knowing that her mother had lived the life afforded by such unimaginable wealth and privilege and then been reduced to such a miserable, degrading existence somehow made her fate worse, and intensified the anger Kat felt towards the man who had refused, up to this point, to acknowledge he even had a granddaughter.

'So, I suppose we're never going to have that movie and take-away night.' Underneath the lightness of his words she glimpsed a genuine sadness that made Kat experience a pang of guilt, acknowledging her own selfishness.

She'd turned to Mike for help, knowing that he wanted to be more than a friend, and had not spared a thought for his feelings. Maybe Zach had been right: she *was* like her grandfather.

Horror at the thought made her respond with more warmth than she might have otherwise shown as she threw her arms around him in a spontaneous bear hug.

'We can keep in touch.'

Zach emerged from the limo to see the embrace. He tensed, his teeth grating together in a white unsmiling barrier as the pressure of outrage building in his chest increased. Waving away the driver and his bags, he kept his eyes trained on the couple, ignoring the whisper in the corner of his brain that suggested his reaction to Katina having a lover was a bit OTT.

The soft sound of her laughter reached his ears, low and *intimate*, he silently translated, feeling the rush of another nameless emotion that pushed him into action, and strode across the concrete. It was nothing to him if she had a lover or a string of them, but the information, he told himself, might have been useful. It wasn't like Alekis to leave out such a detail, so presumably he didn't know about this man either.

He did not doubt that Alekis would manage to separate them, but he found he could see a quicker and more efficient way to facilitate this.

'Good afternoon.'

Furious with herself for jumping guiltily away from Mike at the sound of Zach's voice, she laid a hand on Mike's arm.

'Hello.'

The warmth lacking in her eyes as she had acknowledged the tall Greek's presence was there as she turned back to her friend. 'Mike, this is Zach Gavros. I told you about him.'

She had actually told him very little of what she had learnt online, because, like Sue, Mike's recognition of the name had been instantaneous, though, unlike Sue, Mike's depth of knowledge was more focused on Zach's apparent financial genius than the number of hearts he'd broken. And he hadn't shown the same degree of interest in what the Greek would look like without his shirt as Sue.

Kat, whose Internet trawl had been extensive, and had thrown up pictures of Zach and his ribbed, golden torso on a private beach with a model wearing nothing but a pair of minuscule bikini bottoms, already knew the answer. As she looked at him standing there, in a dark suit topped by a long overcoat, open to reveal his snowy white shirt, she realised that the knowledge of what he looked like minus the tailoring made her cheeks heat.

'This is my friend, Mike Ross.' She tore her eyes from the sensual curve of Zach's mouth and focused on his cleanly shaven jaw while she caught her breath, as Mike stepped forward, hand extended, and for a horrible moment she thought Zach was not going to take it.

'Friend and lawyer. I hope everything was in order, Mr Ross.'

She wasn't surprised that Mike didn't respond. Zach Gavros sounded coldly aloof and slightly bored, and he was already looking over the other man's fair head to a uniformed figure who came across and took Kat's case.

Kat's temper fizzed. The man was rude! To compensate, she bent in and kissed Mike's bearded cheek, her voice huskily emotional as she spoke.

'I'll be in touch.' The warmth faded from her voice as she tilted her head up to the tall, hovering figure. 'Given his form, I needed to know that the money for the refuge is ring-fenced should my *grandfather* decide to chuck *me* out too.'

Zach's eyes narrowed on the beautiful face turned up to him. She was spoiling for a fight but he had no intention of obliging. 'Not the time or place for this conversation, I think—Mr Ross.' The nod was curt as he took her elbow.

She had little choice but to respond to the hand under her elbow. It was either that or be dragged along the concrete. She skipped a little to keep up with his long-legged stride before taking advantage of a slight drop in his pace to snatch her arm away.

Panting, she lifted both hands in an 'enough is enough' gesture as she shook her head. 'Will you slow down? I can't breathe!'

Zach swore under his breath as she started to back away. In seconds she was going to provide the paparazzo he had so far shielded her from with a full-face shot if the two members of his security team zeroing in on the guy, who he knew from experience had the tenacity of a terrier without the charm, didn't reach him in time.

It was a risk Zach was not prepared to take.

He acted on instinct; the question was, *what* instincts?

He moved with speed that bewildered Kat, certainly gave her no opportunity to react as he dragged her with casual ease into his body.

There were no shallows in the kiss. It was hard, deep and possessive. Above the paralyzing shock, on one level she registered the taste of his mouth, the skill of his lips, the hardness of the body so close to her own, but those factors were drowned out by the level that was all shuddering pleasure and heat.

It ended as abruptly as it had begun.

Rocking back on her heels like a sapling in a storm, Kat opened her mouth and no words came. There was a disconnect between her brain and her vocal chords.

'Let's take the "how dare you?" outrage as read,' he drawled, sounding bored and smoothing back his dark hair with a hand that might have held the slightest of tremors as his head turned towards the shouts of protest being issued by the paparazzo as he was escorted away.

Kat followed the line of Zach's gaze, comprehension dawning. The colour rushed to her pale cheeks. *It wasn't as if you thought he'd been overcome by lust for your body, Kat.*

'A shot of me kissing a woman is not worth much.'

'The market being saturated.'

'Whereas the face of a mystery woman fighting me off would be, and that guy may be scum, but he's not stupid,' Zach conceded. 'He has a nose for a story and there were some shots of me leaving the hospital after visiting Alekis. If he had made the link…'

Kat barely heard anything he said after his initial comment. 'I wasn't *fighting* you!'

'Never allow the truth to get in the way of a good headline,' he told her with a cynical smile. 'It's all about perception, trust me, and don't worry, the boyfriend didn't see.'

'He's not my boyfriend, and even if he was that would be none of your business.'

He clicked his long brown fingers. 'In that case, no problem.'

Actually there was, and it was a problem of his

own making. His strategy had been effective but it came with a price tag.

His gaze sank to her lush lips.

The price was the frustration of starting something he couldn't finish, and finishing was obviously a non-starter. It would be a massive betrayal of the trust Alekis had put in him.

His expression concealed by hooded eyelids, he watched as she angrily tapped one foot clad in a spiky little ankle boot. There was an element of compulsion in the slow sweep of his eyes as they travelled up the long smooth curve of her calves covered in dark tights. Not being able to see the outline of her thighs through the kicky little woollen skirt she wore somehow made it more sexy. Imagination was a powerful aphrodisiac.

'Plenty of problems,' she rebutted grimly.

Zach found himself agreeing.

'I do not appreciate being mauled by you whatever the reason.'

'You have a novel way of showing your lack of appreciation.' The memory of how soft and yielding she had felt, how well her curves had fitted into his angles, created a fresh crackle of heat that settled in his groin.

If she had needed a warning that he was dangerous, the slow, predatory half-smile that left his eyes cold would have provided it.

The gesture was casual, his hand did not even

make contact with the skin of her cheek, but it was close enough for her to feel the warmth. She swayed away from it but, warning or not, she had no facility to prevent the image that surfaced in her head. It was a very specific image, sensory in its strength, long brown fingers moving over pale… She escaped the images in her head before she fell over, her breath leaving her parted lips in a raspy gush.

Well, that couldn't be good, could it?

Shame rushed through her as she lifted her chin. There was no way she was going to add herself to the long list of women who had made fools of themselves over Zach Gavros. For starters, she had too much self-respect, and secondly, a much too strongly developed sense of self-preservation.

History would *not* be repeating itself. That was not an option, she told herself, as an image of the sad, overgrown grave flashed into her head. It was an image that represented a life wasted. She was not her mother; *her* hormones were not in charge. If that meant staying a tight, buttoned-up, but safe virgin, it was a price she was happy to pay.

Kat might not know a lot about heart-racing excitement, but she did know she didn't need it and this man was the living embodiment of heart-racing.

His hand dropped; useless to deny this situation was eating into his reserves of self-control.

It was going to get very tiring if he had to remind himself every five minutes that she was Alekis's granddaughter, and as such totally off-limits—a matter not just of respect but practicality.

He needed a distraction, not to mention a release for all the sexual frustration that was clawing low and painfully in his belly, threatening the legendary cool he had long taken for granted. And he knew just the distraction. Andrea Latkis, a very talented and ambitious lawyer on Alekis's Athens-based legal team. Not coy, she had made her desire to sleep with him clear. It was an invitation that he had always intended to accept, but they both had busy lives and their calendars had never been in sync.

It would never have occurred to Andrea to make adjustments to her calendar. He liked that about her, because neither would he, but then maybe drastic situations, or at least uncomfortable ones, required him to make some concessions.

Having come to this conclusion, he was able to experience the rush of heat he endured when Kat removed a glossy strand of hair from her plump lips with something that approached acceptance.

His problem was not Alekis's granddaughter, it was the fact that he had not scheduled a sexual outlet into his life for too long—hence this reaction to having a beautiful woman forcibly thrown into his orbit.

He could relax, though not too much, he cautioned, remembering how he had felt as she'd smiled at the boyfriend. At least there was one interpretation of that moment he could delete—he did not do jealousy.

'Your grandfather is looking forward to meeting you.'

Like ice cream in a heatwave, the antagonism and defiance in her face melted, leaving wide-eyed deer-in-the-headlights fear. He ignored the tightening in his chest that was perilously close to sympathy and looked around.

'Where's the rest of your luggage?'

'I just brought the essentials.'

'For an overnight trip? No matter, we can take your wardrobe in hand when we arrive, and I can arrange to have your belongings shipped over.'

She adopted a calm, no-compromise attitude as she explained, 'No. I intend to keep my London flat on.'

'Alekis has several properties in London. Your things can be moved into whichever you prefer.'

Clearly he had trouble recognising no compromise. 'I prefer my own place, and what do you mean by *take my wardrobe in hand*?' She stopped. She was talking to empty space. Zach had turned and was striding off, his elegant long-legged figure drawing glances to which he seemed utterly oblivious.

She had to trot to catch up with him. 'In hand?' she echoed in a dangerous voice before tacking on breathlessly, 'Will you slow down? We're not all giraffes,' she told him, thinking that a panther was probably a better animal kingdom analogy. His legs might be long but they were in perfect proportion to the rest of his lean, square-shouldered, narrow-hipped frame.

His mouth quirked as he angled a glance down at her lightly flushed face. 'Sorry, I'm not used to—'

She paused as a thoughtful expression flickered across his saturnine features.

'Used to what?'

'Considering anyone else.'

There was nothing even faintly apologetic about his admission. *'Never...?'* Was anyone really that selfish? Kat struggled with the concept.

'You sound shocked.'

'That there are selfish people in the world?' She shook her head. 'I'm not that naive. It's just mostly people try to hide it.'

It wasn't as if he had never been criticised—he'd actually been called a lot worse than selfish—but this was the first time he had ever experienced an inexplicable impulse to defend himself. It wasn't as though her approval meant anything to him— it was an impulse that he firmly crushed as he pushed out coldly, 'There are also virtue-signalling martyrs in the world who, in my experience, rarely try and hide it.'

He heard her sharp intake of breath as she came to an abrupt halt. He took a couple of strides before he stopped and swung back. She was standing there, hands fixed on her hips, her head thrown back as she stared up at him through narrowed amber eyes.

'Are you calling me a martyr?' Her eyelids fluttered as her eyes widened with astonished indignation.

He arched a sardonic brow and heard the sound of her even white teeth grating.

'If you can't take a little constructive criticism, Katina—'

She recognised he was baiting her but not before a strangled *'Constructive!'* had escaped her clenched lips; then she managed a smile of jaw-clenching insincerity. 'Then I suppose I should say thank you, and I promise you that any further *constructive* comments from you on my behaviour will be treated with the same degree of appreciation that I'm feeling now!'

His low, quite impossibly sexy rumble of appreciation—was it possible for a laugh to make you tingle?—had her tumbling from sarcastic superiority back to tingling sexual awareness.

She looked away quickly, embarrassed and confused by her reaction to a laugh, and took a moment before she trusted herself to look up again. When she did the mockery she had come to expect had faded from his lean face, replaced not by sympathy but something that came close to it.

Zach had not got to where he was without possessing an ability to read feelings, so recognising the fear underlying her tough stance was nothing more than he would have expected. What he didn't expect was the surge of irrational guilt attached to the surfacing need to offer her some sort of reassurance.

'I know this must feel frightening, being plunged into an alien environment, but you know, it does us all good to step outside our comfort zone once in a while.' He stopped, his expression closing as he realised how far outside his own comfort zone he was straying. There was a very good reason he didn't wander around emoting. In the financial world, empathy had a way of revealing your own weaknesses.

In his private world it had never been an issue. His relationships, if you chose to call them that, were about sex, not establishing an emotional connection.

The unexpected softening of his tone hit Kat in a weak spot she hadn't even known she had. If he had opened his arms she'd have walked into them wanting...*what*?

When did I turn into the sort of girl who needed a big strong man to turn to?

She let her breath out in a slow, slow hiss, tilted her chin and gave a cool smile. She hadn't turned into that girl and she never would.

'Please don't insult my intelligence by pretending you care,' she snapped back, ignoring the voice in her head that said she was using him as a scapegoat.

The weakness might be hers, but he had exposed it.

'Or do you even know how to spell empathy?'

'Well, if I need to borrow some, I'll know where to come.'

'Meaning?'

'You really are the original bleeding heart. How many men have figured out the way into your bed is by being weak and needy and…*damaged*?' he sneered.

She sucked in an outraged breath through flared nostrils and stalked past him, tossing over her shoulder, 'You are worse than disgusting!'

The sardonic arrogance stamped on his features faded as she walked across the tarmac, her angry posture as graceful as a ballroom dancer's, chin up, her long neck extended, narrow shoulder blades drawn back. He might arguably have won the brief war of words, but the triumph felt hollow. Something possibly to do with the fact his body, reacting independently of his brain, was sending painful slug after slug of raw hunger in response to the movement of her slim body.

Theos, but this woman was killing him, or rather the lusting after her was.

He might consider her out of bounds but there were plenty that wouldn't. His task was getting less enviable with each passing moment.

CHAPTER FIVE

ANY OF THE pleasure Kat might have felt at the sheer novelty value of the travelling style of the rich and famous was ruined for her by the thought of what lay ahead when they landed.

Every time she thought of the man who had left his only daughter to suffer a life a step from the gutter, icy anger rose up in her like a tide. She was not used to such feelings and they made her feel physically sick.

What did he want from her? Forgiveness? A second chance? Kat did not feel she had either in her.

The emotions surging and churning inside her must have shown on her face because at one point during the flight an attendant came and discreetly pointed out the bathroom facilities.

Happy to play along with the assumption she was a poor flyer, Kat vanished in the restroom for a few minutes of solitude she didn't really want—it left too much time for her dark thoughts.

Trailing her hand under the water and looking at herself in the illuminated mirror, she found it easy to understand the attendant's assumption she was about to throw up. She looked terrible, the emotional tussle in her head reflected on her face. She felt bad enough to wish for a foolish split second that Zach, who had fallen into conversation with one of the pilots as they'd boarded and vanished with him, was actually there to distract her—and that was pretty bad!

Nothing as dramatic as the kiss, of course. That had definitely been a step too far, she decided, a dreamy expression drifting into her eyes that she had no control over as she trailed her fingers across the outline of her lips, before snatching them away a moment later with a self-conscious grimace as she realised what she was doing.

When she retook her seat, despite her assuring the attendant she was feeling much better, the woman suggested she should alert Mr Gavros to the situation.

Kat hastily assured her that the only situation was her need to catch up on some sleep.

The attendant reluctantly complied, leaving Kat alone with her own thoughts and her rising sense of panic and trepidation for the rest of the flight. Zach didn't reappear until after they had landed; actually she didn't see him first, she *felt* his presence.

Even though she hadn't looked around she knew the *exact* moment he had appeared. It made her fumble as she released her seat belt and got to her feet, smoothing down her hair and straightening the row of pearly buttons on the square-necked sweater she wore tucked into the belt that emphasised her narrow waist, then stopped because her hands were shaking. The amount of adrenaline circulating in her bloodstream was having a dizzying effect. A situation not improved when she lifted her chin and was no longer able to delay the moment she looked at him.

He had lost the coat and jacket and was standing there, looking elegant and as relaxed as someone as driven as him could. Also, overpoweringly sexy. She blamed the enclosed space and the slight tingle left on her lips from that kiss.

'Where… How…?' She stopped, hating the breathy delivery, and ran a tongue across her dry lips and lifted her chin and husked out, 'Is he… my…*grandfather* here?'

The toughness she had adopted was paper thin; something about the way she stood there looking as vulnerable as hell and too proud to show it awoke something in a tiny, previously dead corner of Zach's heart. He tensed as some nameless emotion clutched at him, making his voice abrupt when he finally responded.

'He's waiting in a hotel next door to the terminal, but don't worry, it'll be private.' Alekis had taken over the penthouse floor to ensure privacy for the meeting, and presumably space for the specialist team on hand with defibrillators.

Zach just hoped this meeting was not going to be memorable for all the wrong reasons.

Her lips tightened. 'I hope he doesn't expect me to pretend, because I won't. I'll tell him what I think of him.'

Her words jolted loose a memory. He remembered saying as much to himself before he'd walked back into the seedy apartment that for seven years had been what some would laughingly call his home. His nostrils flared now as he remembered the sour stale stench that had hit him as he had opened the door.

He was a realist; he hadn't anticipated any sort of an apology or even regret, just an acknowledgement of what they had done. It had become obvious very quickly that he wasn't going to get even that. He'd found his grandmother in her bed, hair matted, unwashed; her eyes had had a vacant look as she'd stared at him without recognition.

Of his uncle there had been no sign. Clearly when free bed and board was not worth the effort of living with a woman with what the doctors had diagnosed as advanced dementia, he had vanished. Later, Zach had discovered he had not got far. It seemed he'd picked a fight with the wrong solitary, weak-looking person, who, it had turned out, had not been alone. His uncle had died of his head injuries three days later—a sordid end to a sordid life.

He pushed away the memory and simultaneously dampened an uncharacteristic need to say something comforting, and almost definitely untrue, to soothe the conflict he could see in those golden eyes.

He couldn't see this meeting being comfortable.

'You mean you can pretend?' He had rarely encountered honesty of the variety she possessed in a world where it was rare for people to speak the truth. She stood out. His eyes slid down her body. She stood out for a lot of reasons.

'He is a stranger and he hurt my mother. He doesn't mean anything to me.'

'Then tell him that. The funding for your refuge is guaranteed.'

Kat found his response bewildering. Was he trying to play devil's advocate? 'You know I can't. He's ill, he might…'

The hand on her shoulder was light but strangely comforting. Finding Zach Gavros comforting in any sense of the word must mean she was in a worse state than she'd thought.

'If I say something and he dies…how am I supposed to live with that?' she choked out.

'Alekis is tough and he has an army of medics on hand. Anything that happens is *not* your responsibility,' he added, suddenly angry as hell with Alekis for putting his granddaughter in this position. 'By this evening you can be swimming in the sea.'

She gave a sudden smile that lightened her expression as she responded to the tip of his head and walked towards the exit. 'That would be something. I can't swim.'

'I'll teach you.' She was looking as startled by the offer as he felt.

'Don't be nice to me or I'll cry.'

'Relax, I'm never nice. Ask anyone. Living on an island, swimming is a necessary survival skill.' As was keeping women like this one an emotional mile away, women who couldn't believe that sex could be just that, women who wanted something deeper and more meaningful, women who needed an emotional depth he simply didn't have.

It was an exaggeration to say the hotel was next door to the airport, but it was conveniently close.

'It's very nice,' she said, keeping up the same flow of polite conversation she had during the car transfer. It helped maintain the illusion of normality but was, she realised, starting to sound desperate.

Actually, the hotel, part of a luxury chain she had vaguely heard of, was *extremely* nice in a plush, upmarket way.

'Thank you.'

She threw a questioning look up at Zach's austerely handsome profile. 'The chain is a relatively recent purchase. It was a bit tired, but it's amazing what a refurb can do.'

'You own it?' Well, that explained the manager who was rushing out to greet them before personally escorting them to the private entrance to the penthouse floor, where the elevator door was flanked by men wearing suits and dark glasses who spoke into the headsets they were wearing.

Kat hesitated before she stepped inside the lift, taking a moment to pull her shoulders back and lift her chin.

Stepping in after her, Zach felt a twinge of admiration. It was impossible not to. She looked as though she were walking into a lion's den, but, my God, she was doing it with style!

The swishing upward ride took seconds and then the doors were silently opening.

'He is as nervous as you.'

Kat lifted her eyes. 'I seriously doubt that. I feel like I used to when I hid.' She had always had a hiding place ready when the loud voices had started, a place to crawl into and try to be invisible.

No hiding place now, Kat! Just do it!

He sensed she had not even realised what she had said, words that might not have made sense to many but, as someone who had tried very hard to be invisible, he knew that she was talking of an experience similar to, but he *really* hoped not the same as, his own.

He found himself hoping grimly that the mother who had abandoned her had retained enough motherly feeling to protect her child from violence, the sort that had scarred his own youth.

The golden eyes lifted to his. 'I'm afraid I won't be able to stop myself, that I'll say something really bad—I'm so angry,' she whispered, pressing a hand to her breastbone as if to physically hold in the storm of emotions raging there.

'Don't be afraid. You've a right to be angry.' Maybe she would have the apologies and explanations he'd been robbed of.

'I thought you were team Alekis.' *He has a beautiful mouth*... The thought drifted through the tangled knot of thoughts in her head as she stared at the sensually carved lines... Had he *really* kissed her? The memory, like everything else, had an unreal quality.

'You won't say anything to hurt him. You're too...*kind*.' He allowed himself the comment because he spoke as an objective observer. He was not here to get involved in the relationship between grandfather and granddaughter. He carried the inescapable taint of his own family with him through life without getting involved in someone else's family conflict.

The way he said *kind*, he made it sound like a defect—not that Kat felt kind as her attention narrowed in on the figure seated in a large chair that made her think of a throne, placed centre stage in the room.

She'd seen photos online, but this man was older, much older, yet even with a craggy face, drawn, with fatigue deepening the shadowy bags beneath his eyes, you could sense the power coming off the man. Then, a second later, she saw the eyes beneath the thick white eyebrows were filled with tears.

The wave of emotion that hit her was so unexpected and so powerful that all the other emotions seething inside her were swallowed up. This was her grandfather—her family.

'Katina?'

She pressed a hand to her trembling lips as the figure in the chair held out his arms. 'I am so s-sorry, Katina.'

Zach watched her fight to hold on to her antagonism and fail.

Even the relatively short time he had spent in her company meant that it didn't cross Zach's mind that her capitulation had anything at all to do with personal gain. This was about her generous spirit, and her longing for a family, or at least her idea of what a family was.

She was homesick for an idea.

The world called Zach reckless, a risk taker with a golden touch, but it was a lie. He never risked anything he was not willing to lose. Money was not important to him in itself. Lose a fortune, make a fortune—these were not things that would ever keep him awake. They were challenges, a test of mental agility.

True recklessness was what she possessed. It was the open-hearted way she ran towards the possibility of family and love, risking having her illusions shattered.

Zach admired it, and it appalled him.

Was he team Alekis? No, but neither was he the objective observer he wanted to be. Somehow this woman had awoken a protective instinct in him. He didn't want to feel this way as he watched her cover the space between her and the old man, before dropping with graceful spontaneity to her knees beside the chair.

He turned abruptly and left, reminding himself that he was not part of this drama as he stepped into the elevator, pushing away feelings he didn't want to name, let alone feel.

Part of Kat didn't want to let go of her anger: it felt like a betrayal to her mother, but it had gone, burned away in that explosion of feeling. She'd practised her cold words but how could she be mean when he looked so frail and sounded so tearfully penitent? Though she got a glimpse of the iron man who people feared when he imperiously waved away someone who appeared to check his blood pressure.

A moment later the first man came back with reinforcements. Several nurses in uniform and the dapper figure in the three-piece suit did not react to the scowl directed at him.

'I really must insist. These readings…'

For the first time, Kat realised that there were leads trailing under her grandfather's suit, which were presumably giving readings in the connecting room.

'All right—all right!'

Kat wondered if his capitulation had anything to do with the beads of sweat along his upper lip when he caught her hand.

'As I was saying, it is a small gathering. Nothing too formal, drinks and mingling…'

Saying? she thought, playing catch up. She couldn't recall him saying anything about a *gathering*, but then the short, emotionally charged conversation was a bit of a blur.

'A small press presence…'

Her heart started to pound and she felt sick.

'Don't worry, they are friendly, all invited. One

of the advantages of owning an island is that it is easier to keep out undesirable guests.' The claw-like hand tightened on her own, crushing her fingers. 'You're an Azaria, you'll be fine.'

The medics closed in, wielding scary-looking syringes, and she backed away, unable to tell him that she *wasn't* an Azaria and she didn't fit into this life.

As she walked into the lift, the feeling of sick unease in the pit of her stomach grew. What had she just agreed to? Had she agreed to anything? She didn't want to go to a *gathering*, whatever that meant, formal or otherwise.

As the lift doors opened, Zach peeled himself away from the wall he had been leaning against and stood there, hands in his pockets, looking at her.

'You look like you need a drink.' And maybe a hug? He banished the aberrant thought. He was not a *huggy* person, and with Kat hugs would not stay comforting for long. His long fingers flexed as he saw the image in his head of them sliding under that top and over her warm skin.

'I'd prefer a few explanations. Gathering? Press?'

'Ah.'

'So you know what this is about?' She wasn't sure if she was relieved or resentful.

'Basically we are talking cocktail party. Alekis invites a few tame journalists a few times a year, lets them mingle with what is actually quite an eclectic bunch—'

Her voice, shrill with panic, cut across him. 'I can't mingle.'

He didn't look impressed. 'Rubbish. Here's the car now.'

She shook her head. 'No. I'm not going anywhere until you tell me what is going on.'

'We need to control the flow of information. Denying rumours will only—'

Her eyes flew wide in alarm. 'What rumours?'

His eyes lifted. 'A story will appear tomorrow confirming that your grandfather had a heart attack. This is a story that would normally dominate headlines for weeks, excite a predictably hysterical reaction and hit market confidence.'

'You couldn't stop this story?' Kat felt a bit guilty that she was relieved this was about market confidence and not about her.

There was a ruthless quality to the thin-lipped smile he gave in response that made her shiver. 'I planted the story.'

The addition of *obviously* was silent, but quite definitely there. Confused by that as much as his admission, she shook her head. 'But you just said—' she began, feeling her way.

'I said *normally*. On this occasion Alekis's illness will be buried by the much more exciting information that he has been united with his long-lost granddaughter.'

'So, you're using me.'

She sounded shocked by the discovery. His dark brows flattened into a line of exasperation above his obsidian stare.

'This was not my idea.' He wasn't trying to deflect her anger, but he decided it might be a good thing that she recognised that even at death's door her grandfather was not a warm and cuddly person.

It was bizarre he had to spell it out, but despite her upbringing, inexplicably it seemed to come as a shock to her that anyone had motives that were not pure and elevated.

He wasn't going to be the only one to notice her lack of guile and sophistication, but he might be the only one who wasn't trying to use it to his own advantage. You did not have to be psychic to predict that if she didn't toughen up, and quick, she was going to be a soft touch for every hard-luck sob story going. He hoped for her sake she was a quick learner, or else she was in for some painful lessons in human nature.

She glanced towards the building behind them. 'He?'

'Alekis delegated, but yes, the plan is his. It's nothing sinister. We're controlling the flow of information. Or would you prefer some tabloid breaks the story, sensationalising it? Perhaps digging up an old lover to publish a kiss-and-tell?' He saw no benefit from telling her that this might happen anyway. There were going to be disgruntled ex-lovers coming out of the woodwork once the news of the heiress hit. 'This way your exposure is controlled. Hiding you away would have photographers in helicopters flying over Tackyntha with telephoto lenses.'

Her startled eyes looked up at him as she slid into the car. 'People will want to take my photograph?' she said as he joined her.

'Are you trying to be facile?'

She shook her head.

He sighed and pushed his head into the leather headrest. 'Belt up, Katina.'

She did and sat there looking shell-shocked.

Zach waited until the car moved away and into the traffic before he spoke. 'You are going to be one of the wealthiest women in Europe, Katina. People will all want to know what you had for breakfast, what your favourite colour nail varnish is. They will discuss what you're wearing and speculate on your sexuality, whether you have an eating disorder or a drug problem.'

He watched as the horror of the reality hit home, feeling like a bastard, but better a bastard on her side than one who could exploit the vulnerability on display in her wide eyes and trembling lips.

She half rose in her seat before subsiding, no parachute, no escape—*no escape*. 'Oh, God!' she groaned, closing her eyes. 'I can't do this.'

'Yes, you can.'

His firm, unsympathetic rebuttal made her eyes fly wide as she directed a glare of simmering dislike at him. She had seen lumps of granite with more empathy than he possessed.

'The way you handle yourself these first few weeks is important, will set a pattern. Alekis's wealth means people don't have automatic access to you. I can put up some barriers to protect you.'

She pushed away the images of walls around a gold-lined cage that flashed through her head, telling herself not to be such a drama queen. There was plenty to be nervous about without inventing things.

'You hide away and people will assume you have something to hide. We need to create the illusion you are open,' he explained, digging deep into his reserves of patience as he explained what was obvious. 'While telling them essentially nothing.'

Her dark feathered brows lifted. *'We?'*

'All right, you. One of the first things you need to remember is trust no one, *no one*,' he emphasised grimly. 'Not *everyone* you meet will be out for a piece of you,' he conceded.

'Just ninety per cent of them. What a relief!' She quivered. He was really selling this lifestyle.

'I'm not stupid, you know. I might even be able to work out which knife and fork to use. I am a fast learner.'

'That remains to be seen. I won't pretend it isn't going to be a steep learning curve.'

'Oh, I really wish you would pretend that it is.'

He responded to her attempt at humour with a hard look. 'But you will learn to judge. Learn your own style. Until you do, that's what I'm here for.'

She fixed him with a narrow-eyed glare. 'So you mean you'll put the words in my mouth and tell me what to wear.' She folded her arms across her chest and directed a belligerent stare up at his face. 'I'm not a puppet.'

'No. From where I'm sitting you are...' He completed the sentence in a flood of angry-sounding Greek before finally dragging a hand through his dark hair as he sat there, lips compressed, dark eyes burning.

'I don't understand Greek.'

'I said,' he gritted out, 'I am trying to protect you, but if you would prefer I throw you to the wolves...?'

As their eyes connected, glittering black on gold, a strange little shiver traced a slow, sinuous path up her tension-stiffened spine.

'What is this? Set a thief to catch a thief, or in this case a wolf to catch a wolf?' It was true, there was definitely something of the lean, feral predator about him, which she could see might appeal to some women.

'For your information, I have not spent my life in a protective bubble and I've been coping without a guardian angel—which, for the record, is *definitely* major miscasting—all my life. I resent being treated like a child.'

Were you ever a child? he wondered as his glance moved in an unscheduled slow sweep over her slim, tense figure, oozing hostility, before coming to rest on the outline of her lips. The dull throb in his temples got louder as he saw faceless wolves drawn to the delicious invitation of their plump pinkness.

The barrier of his clenched teeth did nothing to shield him from a fresh onslaught of painful desire. Alekis had put him in a 'rock and hard place' position. He couldn't lay a finger on her without betraying the trust the older man had, for some reason, placed in him and he couldn't walk away, either.

'So, we are going to the island.'

'It doesn't take long by helicopter.'

Kat felt reluctant to admit she'd never flown in one. 'And do your family live there too? Is that how you know Alekis?'

A look she couldn't quite put a name to flickered in his eyes. It was gone so quickly that she might have imagined it.

'No, my family do not live there.'

'But you have family…?' she asked, remembering how he had spoken about his mother's death. 'They were there for you after your mother died?'

'You think because our mothers are dead that gives us something in common? It does not.'

She flushed. If he'd tried to embarrass her, he'd succeeded. Did he think she didn't know they came from two different worlds? That she needed him to point out they had nothing in common, that he had been raised in a world of wealth and privilege that she knew she would never fit into.

Being orphaned was always an awful thing for any child, but in Zach's world there were cushions…nannies, good schools. None could replace maternal love, but it helped if you had the support structure of a family, especially one that meant you didn't stand out because your clothes were not the latest fashion, or you had no holiday to talk about at the start of a new school term.

'You really do worry about family, don't you? Well, relax—yes, I *did* have family.' His lips curled in a cynical smile of remembrance. 'An uncle who is now happily dead and a grandmother who is a great deal pleasanter now that she doesn't remember my name, or, for that matter, her own.'

Shock reverberated through his body, none of it showing on his still shuttered face as he realised he had just revealed more to her than he had to another living person. Not even Alekis knew the details about his life before they had met, and here he was spilling his guts to this woman, with her ridiculous sentimentality, virtually inviting her to walk around in his head!

Was this a new symptom of sexual deprivation?

She looked at his bleakly beautiful face and felt her heart squeeze with sympathy. His comment had been sparing in detail, but you didn't need to have worked with children caught in the firing line of family conflict to recognise that Zach's childhood had not been what she'd imagined.

'I'm so sorry,' she said, wondering uneasily how many of her other assumptions about him were wrong.

'There is no need to be sorry,' he sliced back coldly. 'It is the past.'

Did he really believe it was that easy? she wondered, remembering all the times when she was growing up that she had wished that her past were a painless blank. That she didn't have the snatches of memories that made her sad, while filling her with a nameless longing.

Glancing at his shuttered face, she recognised that she had pushed him as far as she could on the subject. She changed tack. 'So, what is your connection to Alekis?'

'I wonder about that sometimes myself.'

Before she could voice her frustration at this

deliberately unhelpful response, he added, 'Your grandfather helped me when no one else would.'

'So, a financial loan…?' she probed.

His eyes were hidden by his half-lowered lids but the smile that quivered on his sensually sculpted mouth intrigued her. 'Not as such, but I remain in your grandfather's debt. I doubt very much if I would be where I am today without his intervention.'

'Where would you be?'

'I sometimes ask myself that, but not often. I prefer to deal with the here and now, and in the here and now I consider myself in Alekis's debt.'

'Do you like him?'

His dark brows drew together in a straight line above his aquiline nose. 'He has many qualities I admire and many faults I accept.' His dark eyes had a mesmeric quality as he captured her gaze and there was an intensity in his words as he spoke. 'The door to the world you are about to enter is rarely opened to outsiders. I was an outsider, so maybe Alekis thought I was well placed to help your transition.'

'So you're not an outsider now?'

'I have never been a joiner.'

Did he *ever* give a straight answer? she wondered. 'But you want me to join.'

He shook his head. 'That will be your choice.

I want you to be aware of the pitfalls. To learn how to—'

'Blend in?'

He gave a sudden laugh, deep and uninhibited. It melted his expression into a smile that made him look years younger and made the bottom of her stomach dissolve. She realised that if this man ever made the effort to charm there wasn't a woman alive who could resist.

Including me!

Now there was a fact to keep her awake at nights.

'What is so funny?'

'The idea of you blending in anywhere.' The laughter died from his face, leaving something much darker, much more intense, more dangerous, she realised, than mere charm. 'You're an exceptionally beautiful woman.'

His deep voice was like rumpled velvet, warm, sensuous and will-sapping. She had no idea how long she sat there staring at him before the blare of a car horn jolted her back to reality.

The reality being that Zach possessed a voice that really ought to carry a danger warning! Ah, well, the next time, should there be a next time, she would be prepared and not look like such an idiot.

She broke the seductive hold of his dark, mesmerising stare, though the effort filmed her skin

with sweat as she snapped out contemptuously,
'Don't be stupid!'

Obviously she knew she wasn't *bad* to look at,
but *exceptionally beautiful* was not a term used
for a woman who had a mouth that was way too
big for her face, a gap between her front teeth and
the sort of body that looked great in clothes but
without them… She hated her bony collarbones
and she didn't see how anyone could consider the
visible angles on her hips feminine.

Her reaction to him stating the obvious seemed
strange. You could be excused for assuming, given
her reaction, that no one had ever told her how
beautiful she was before. Even if she had had lov-
ers who left a lot to be desired, he thought scornfully, the woman had a mirror.

'Even if you could blend in you shouldn't. You
should carry on being yourself, as much as is possible.'

She looked bemused by the advice. 'Who else
would I be? I think you worry too much. I'm used
to being the odd one out. The kid in care with the
wrong clothes.'

If the comment had been made in an attempt to
garner sympathy, Zach would not have felt any. He
did not *want* to now, and yet as he looked at her
he experienced less sympathy but a sudden deep
anger for the childhood she had been robbed of.

And yet she seemed to have her own set of values that nobody had been able to take from her.

Could he say the same? *Maybe she had come to terms with her past more than he had his?*

He pushed the thought away; the past was something he did have to come to terms with. It was gone and buried. Not only could he not imagine himself discussing it so openly as she did, but he could not imagine wanting to.

CHAPTER SIX

'YOU CAN OPEN your eyes now. We're in the air.'

She did so, taking a breath and realising that at some point during the take off she had grabbed his hand and dug her nails in hard.

With a self-conscious 'Sorry... ' she released it, her brows twitching into a front of dismay as she saw the half-moon crescents standing out white in his olive skin. Pretending to tuck a stray strand of hair behind her ears, she rubbed the skin of her cheek, which was tingling from the warm brush of his breath. It was scary that her body was so sensitive to him.

'I've never been in a helicopter before.'

She just hoped the transfer would be as short as he had promised. Kat leaned forward in her seat to loosen the hair that had got caught down the neck of her sweater. As she leaned back, her glance connected with Zach's.

The lurch in her stomach had nothing to do with their mode of transport as the moment that vibrated with unseen electricity stretched. He was sitting close enough for her to see the network of fine lines that fanned out from the corners of his eyes and the dusting of dark stubble shading his jaw, the shadow adding extra emphasis to the hollows of his cheeks.

She breathed a little deeper, unconsciously leaning forward as her nostrils flared, picking up on the clean male scent that rose from his warm skin. Sensations she had no name for shifted inside her and she paused, like someone standing on the edge of quicksand, fighting the urge to jump in with both feet.

Just before she reached tipping point, she jerked back again abruptly. The sudden adrenaline rush continued to make her head spin. She flexed her fingers before closing both hands tight, trying not to think of that unacknowledged moment when she had been within a heartbeat of reaching out and touching his cheek. It had been an instinctive thing. Kat would have been happier not knowing she possessed such instincts.

And *much* happier not having the image in her head of them lying naked together. Shame mingled with real fear as she dragged her eyes away from the firm sensual line of his mouth. Maybe there was a faulty gene responsible for being attracted to bad men…and she had inherited it? It had always been her secret fear.

Zach's eyes were hooded as he watched her, reminding himself that the task assigned him by Alekis was keeping men out of her bed, not occupying it himself. It did not assuage the ache in his groin as he watched her pupils tellingly dilate until only a thin ring of amber remained.

The muscles in Zach's brown throat rippled as he swallowed, his heavy lids lowered over his eyes as he turned his head to direct his hooded stare out of the window. He had not experienced this sort of elemental response to a woman in a long time and knowing she felt the same attraction, when they were sitting this close and she was looking at him with those hungry eyes, was not making his life any easier.

He closed his eyes to shut out the temptation, but the ache in his body did not diminish as he breathed his way through the hot elemental surge of raw desire that he had to endure because he sure as hell had no control over it.

Kat sat there, heart pounding, throat dry, wondering if he was going to acknowledge the crackle of sexual tension that shimmered in the air between them or even do something about it. Trying to decide if she wanted him to or not.

She was actually on the point of saying something, exactly what she didn't know, when he closed his eyes, and within seconds gave the impression of man deeply asleep.

She had worked herself up into a state of breathless anticipation and he was asleep!

Her cheeks stung pink with mortified heat when she realised how close she had come to utterly humiliating herself. It had felt so real, so tangible. Had it *really* been in her imagination? she wondered, studying the strong lines on his face. Sleep had ironed out some of the austerity and hardness from his face and made him seem younger somehow.

It really was odd to find yourself attracted to someone you did not even like; in fact, actively disliked, she mused, suddenly sleepy herself as the tensions of the last few hours began to catch up with her. Perhaps the *odd* thing was that she had never felt this way before.

Or maybe *she* was just the oddity, a virgin because she'd never allowed anyone to get close enough to change the situation. There had been moments of uncomfortable self-awareness when she'd recognised that this was in part at least due to her deep-seated fear of abandonment, but it was an insight she pushed away.

The same way she'd been pushing away the glaringly obvious fact that she was attracted to Zach Gavros. Of course, denial had been a lot easier when she had been able to think of him as an arrogant two-dimensional figure, but getting a glimpse of his vulnerabilities was making that a lot harder.

Would these newly aroused feelings go back into hibernation once Zach vanished from her life?

Did she want them to?

Kat hadn't worked out the answer by the time her eyelids flickered closed and did not lift.

She knew it was a dream—she'd had it before many times, but not for a long time now. The heart-thudding, stomach-clenching sense of icy dread. Except it wasn't *her*—it was someone else she was watching, crouched small in her hiding place, waiting for the monster's hand to reach in and drag her out. Kat wanted to shout a warning to the little girl, but her voice wouldn't work. Her entire body felt paralysed. She was watching, waiting, helpless to stop what was about to happen.

I'm asleep...asleep...it's not real. She kept repeating the words in her head, fighting her way through the grey layers of sleep to the surface. The process was all consuming, exhausting, then she heard a sound and focused on it, dragging herself clear of the shadows.

As she opened her eyes an indistinct face seemed to be floating there. She watched the outline grow more defined and more solid. Zach was leaning forward in his seat, talking to her.

'We have arrived.'

She blinked, had a moment utter blank, before the memories all came rushing back. She pulled herself upright in her seat with a jerk. 'Oh, God! I must have fallen asleep.' She dragged her hands over her slippery, silky hair, anchoring stray tips behind her ears as she smoothed it.

'You were dreaming.'

'Was I?' she said, thinking, *You were watching me...* and feeling quite extraordinarily exposed.

'You don't remember?'

He was looking at her with what felt like uncomfortable intensity. 'Who remembers dreams?' she said, turning her head to look out of the window, determined that whatever she saw, if her grandfather ate off gold plates and showered in champagne, she was not going to display unworldly awe. She'd show Zach she could pretend as well as anyone.

Her decision incinerated at her first glimpse of her new island home. Temporary home, reminded the voice of caution in her head.

It helped that their arrival coincided with the start of a breathtaking sunset, which, as they came in to land, had just tinged the water with feathers of red.

The landing strip seemed close to the candy-coloured village with terracotta roofs they had flown over, appearing to be cut into the rock of a peninsula that projected into the sea. She doubted her grandfather's villa could be set anywhere more spectacular.

She glanced towards the backdrop of green

mountains, looking for signs of a road that might lead to the villa.

'Is it far?' she asked, releasing her white-knuckled grip on the armrest and willing her stomach to stop churning as the helicopter set down and she released the breath held in her chest in a long sibilant sigh of relief.

He angled a questioning look at her face. 'Far?'

'To the house, villa, whatever—is it far from the village?'

An amused smile deepened the lines fanning out from his deep-set eyes. 'There is no village.'

'Town, then,' she said, irritated by his pedantic response.

'Not one of those, either.'

'But…' Her brows twitched into a frown. 'I saw…' Comprehension dawned and her eyes flew wide. 'You're telling me that was a *house*?'

The incredulous uplift of her voice on the word made his lips twitch.

'But where are the people?'

'There is a live-in staff, obviously.'

Still in shock, she watched as he turned to someone who had entered the helicopter; presumably the younger man had been waiting for their arrival. He tipped his head towards Kat and spoke at length in Greek with Zach, who responded in the same language, saying something that had the other man smiling and heading for the exit.

Zach turned his eyes, stilling on her averted face. She was struggling to loosen the clip on her safety restraint. A hank of hair had fallen across her face and he experienced the strangest impulse to push it back. Would the skin of her cheek be as smooth and soft as it appeared?

His hands clenched into fists as though they held the silky tendrils, before he brought the line of speculation to an abrupt halt. The fact that the questions had been there to begin with was a massive wake-up call. Just a warning; he was in control and in no danger of losing it now.

If the thought lacked conviction, he refused to acknowledge it. Admitting it would have meant acknowledging a chink in his armour.

Freeing herself after a tussle, Kat lifted her head and found he was looking at her with an intensity that made her stomach flip. For a moment the charge in the air, imaginary or real, was back, and it took her breath away before, heart thudding, she managed to lower her lashes in a self-protective shield. Had she imagined that moment? Had it been a creation of her over-heated imagination? *Wishful thinking?*

The sly whisper vanished like smoke but not before her spine had stiffened in utter rejection, that she would want to unleash anything in him let alone… A tiny little shudder showered through her body as she moistened her dry lips. It was ludicrous, more than ludicrous, she told herself firmly, laughable!

Only she wasn't laughing.

'Your grandfather bought the island in the sixties, I believe. At the time there was a church, a couple of houses, but the only occupants were the goats. A goatherd came over from the mainland once every couple of weeks to tend them. So no evictions. The goats are still here too, but don't try hugging them. They are feral creatures, not tame, so approach with caution.'

Kat stared at his face. In profile, there was a strength to the angles and planes that touched her now that she'd told herself it was a purely aesthetic level of appreciation.

Yes, he was beautiful to look at, but he was also *not tame.*

Luckily, she had never been drawn to the untamed, or unpredictable.

There you go with the denial again, Kat, taunted the voice in her head. *Afraid you've got more of your mother in you than you admit to?*

'All right.' She set her shoulders. 'So what now?'

'Now I escort you to the villa and introduce you to your new home.'

Standing up, her head ducked, she followed him towards the open doors.

CHAPTER SEVEN

THE TWO CARS, the first carrying the minimal baggage and the second themselves, drew up onto the illuminated forecourt. Night had fallen with a speed she found confusing, a clear starlit night scented with the smell of the sea and wild thyme.

Zach, who had gone around to open her door, left her to the assistance of the driver and moved forward to meet the woman who appeared in the massive set of double doors that were flung open to welcome them.

Dressed in a tailored black dress that suited her curvy figure, the woman was average height. It was hard to tell from this distance if the silver streaks in her dark hair were natural or a fashion statement. The chignon it was arranged in appeared as smooth and immaculate as the rest of her.

Kat felt travel-worn and untidy by comparison. She tucked the stray strands of hair behind her ears and told herself if she started worrying about what impression she made on everyone here she'd be a nervous wreck within the week.

Zach's voice drifted across the space to Kat; it sounded warm.

'Selene.'

As she watched from where she stood beside the car it seemed to Kat there was a genuine affection in his greeting as he put his hands on the shoulders of the woman, who Kat judged to be in her forties, and kissed her cheeks.

The rapid interchange was in Greek, and, as the woman glanced over in her direction several times, it didn't seem paranoid to assume they were discussing her.

Get used to it, Kat, she told herself as they began to walk back towards her.

'Katina, this is Selene Carras, your grandfather's housekeeper. This, Selene, is—'

'You have a look of Mia, my dear.'

Kat's cautiously polite expression melted in wondering disbelief. Eyes sparking eagerness, she sounded incredulous. 'You *knew* my mother?'

'Indeed I did.' The smartly dressed woman's kind brown eyes crinkled deeply at the corners as she smiled, her teeth as white as the double row of pearls around her neck. 'My own mother was the housekeeper on the island before me. When we were girls your mother and I would play together during her school holidays before we got older and…she was missed greatly by many.'

Emotion filled Kat's throat. There had never been anyone in her life she could speak to about her mother, never anyone she could ask all the questions she wanted, *needed* to ask.

'She used to tell me stories when I was little about an island where the sun always shone and the sand on the beaches was white. I thought they were stories. I never thought…' When her throat clogged with unshed tears of emotion, she turned her head, blinking hard, embarrassed less by the overspill of emotion than by the fact Zach was witnessing it.

Though, ironically, it was Zach who unwittingly came to her rescue.

'Did I hear dinner mentioned?'

'Of course, Mr Zach, but first things first. I will show Miss—'

'Kat, please,' Kat begged, not caring if this was etiquette or not.

The woman tipped her head. 'I will show Kat to her rooms, give her time to freshen up and then I'll have dinner served in half an hour?' She glanced from Kat to Zach, taking their silence as agreement, and continued cheerfully. 'Mr Zach will bring you down to dinner.' She glanced at him before explaining. 'The house is not exactly compact and it takes a little time to get your bearings.'

Not compact!

If the hallway they entered was any indication, the place was massive!

Underfoot the marble glowed while, high above, the massive antique chandeliers glistened. The central sweeping staircase ran up to the gallery above and then upwards to another floor.

It was Zach's voice, deep and inflected with dry irony, that interrupted her shocked silence.

'Alekis is not really a fan of less is more, and he really thinks that size matters. There isn't a room in the place that you couldn't have a game of cricket in. Well, not really my game, but…'

'It didn't stop you trying.' The older woman touched Kat's arm. 'The rooms *are* a little large.'

Kat only dimly registered the interchange.

'Ah.' Zach breathed and paused when he saw what had stopped her in her tracks.

'She is beautiful,' Kat said, staring.

'Your grandmother, I believe.'

Kat, her eyes wide, glanced at him and then back at the portrait in the heavy gold frame. It was positioned on the far wall lit by several spotlights. She took a step closer to study the woman, one she had never met or even knew existed.

This woman was her grandmother.

The roots she had been longing for all her life, Kat realised, were here. But did she belong? This was all so alien.

'My grandmother?'

The woman in the painting was wearing a classic shift dress that would have looked fashionable today, the knee-high boots elongated her legs and her dark hair was dressed in a slightly bouffant updo. With her dark eyes outlined by kohl, her rosebud lips pale and her lashes spiky and long, it was an iconic sixties look.

'She looks like Mum…' The face that she thought she remembered floated into her head. 'I *think*?'

Zach could not see her face, just hear the almost quiver in her voice, but it was the set of her narrow shoulders and the emotions he could feel literally radiating from her that made something twist hard in his chest. Something he refused to recognise as tenderness. An equally unfamiliar impulse to offer comfort made him move forward.

He had been so focused on the solitary figure staring up at the painting that he didn't realise he wasn't the only one affected by the poignant image she made, until the housekeeper wrapped her plump arm around the younger woman's slender shoulders. The touch was brief but enough to draw a smile of warm gratitude from Kat as the older woman moved away.

Spontaneous expressions of support and comfort were not really in Zach's comfort zone. Far better, he decided, watching the moment, to leave it to those with more experience with touchy-feely stuff. Despite his ineligibility he found the feeling that he'd been cheated out of the feel of her warm skin lingering, digging deep enough to make him ache. Everything between them seemed to come back to one thing: this desire that never quite went away and flared in an unpredictable way. Problematic but not anything he couldn't deal with—he had never allowed his appetites to rule him.

The housekeeper studied the portrait. 'She did, more so as she grew up.'

Kat sent her another look of teary gratitude. 'I don't have any photos, just what I remember, and I'm not sure how much of that is real,' she admitted.

Listening, Zach found himself wanting to tell her she was lucky; he wished his own memories of his childhood were open to misinterpretation, but his were all unpleasantly real.

'This way.'

'I'll show her the way,' he heard himself say.

'Really?' Selene shook her head and recovered her poise. 'Of course.'

'This is a lot for you to take in.'

Kat nodded. 'Pretty overwhelming. Until now I hadn't thought of my mother being here, not really.' She stopped as her throat closed over, not conscious that Zach had slowed to keep pace with her. 'Do you remember your mother?'

Midway up the sweeping staircase, he stopped. Puzzled by his rigid posture, so did Kat.

'Yes,' he said finally, and began to walk again.

'I wish I remembered more.'

He stopped again, this time at the top of the staircase, and looked down at her, his expression sombre.

'Be careful what you wish for.'

He *remembered*; he remembered a once beautiful woman worn down by single parenthood and the two or three jobs she'd needed to pay the rent on their apartment and keep him in clothes. She had always been tired, and Zach remembered promising her that one day she would not have to work. He would have a job that meant she could rest; rest had seemed like the ultimate luxury.

He never got the chance; he was ten when she died. For years he'd assumed it had been the exhaustion that had taken her life, a life that had been a constant, unrelenting grind. Only later he'd learnt by accident when he'd found her death certificate that she had succumbed to pneumonia. In her weakened condition she hadn't been able to fight the infection that had ravaged her body or afford the medicine that might have saved her.

Unable to explain even to herself this *need* in her to know more about him, more about the man who wore power so comfortably, she tentatively pushed. 'After your mother died you went to live with your grandmother, and—?'

'Dimitri, my uncle.'

The bleakness in his voice was reflected in his face as he continued to speak. She had the impression that he had almost forgotten she was there as he continued.

'If she could love anyone, she loved him, in her way, though of course that love came a poor second to the bottom of a vodka bottle.'

'She didn't love you?' The question slipped out. She knew it was one she had no right to ask but anger pushed it through her caution.

'Me?' He laughed, the sound hard. 'She resented me almost as much as she had resented her own daughter. She forgot I was there for the most part and left me to Dimitri. Dimitri was a weak man who blamed the world for anything that went wrong in his life, and, like many weak men who could not take responsibility for their own actions, he was a bully. He used me as a punching bag.'

Kat felt the tears press against the back of her eyelids. He remembered every blow, every curse. She knew it without him telling her.

'I hate bullies!'

Her fierce declaration brought his eyes back to her face as she stood there, her hands clenched into fists, the empathy shining clear in her glorious eyes. He froze. What the *hell* had he just done?

What had begun as a lesson in caution had become some sort of soul-baring session. Feelings that he had put into cold storage had been resurrected. His jaw clenched. He had every intention of putting them safely back behind the mental ten-foot-high steel-reinforced walls that had taken him years of painstaking effort to construct.

'I remembered…' The housekeeper's voice drifted up the deep stairwell and they both turned as she mounted the first few steps.

Kat tore her eyes off Zach's curiously expressionless face.

The older woman, standing at the bottom step, was breathing hard as though she'd just run back.

'You mentioned photos—I have some. They are mostly from a few summers. I will look them out for you,' she promised. 'There used to be lots about the place.'

'Thank you,' Kat called down, genuinely touched by the gesture.

'This way,' Zach said, indicating the corridor to the left. He sounded distant and cold. She was assuming he was regretting opening up to her. It was pretty obvious he was not a man who was into sharing his feelings.

'So what happened to the photos of my mother?'

'Before my time,' he said abruptly, before adding, 'I'm not sure, but your grandfather will know.'

Unless he'd destroyed them, Kat thought, imagining the angry man trying to wipe his daughter from his life. The thought left her feeling deflated as she walked beside a silent Zach down what seemed like several miles of corridors until Zach stopped at a door.

'You're here.' As he spoke a maid emerged from the room. She seemed flustered when she saw them.

Zach said something in Greek that made her smile and tip her head towards the room and say something in her native tongue before moving away.

'What did she say?' Kat asked.

'You're not going to learn if I keep translating for you.'

Kat, who had turned to follow the girl's progress down the wide corridor, turned back to Zach. He was a lot closer than she had anticipated. She took a hasty step backwards, nothing to do with retreat and a lot to do with self-preservation. His *closeness* had a disturbing effect on her nervous system.

'So how am I going to learn? Or is that the idea—to make me feel like an outsider?' She regretted the self-pitying addition the moment it left her lips, but in reality she felt as though she always would be an outsider here. It seemed impossible that she would ever fit in.

'You could take lessons.'

She noticed he didn't offer.

'Though they say immersion's the best way to learn a language.'

'Who's they?' she jeered, unimpressed.

'Experts.'

She snapped her fingers to express her opinion of experts. 'I call it stupid, a bit like saying throwing someone in the deep end is the best way to learn to swim.'

'But you can't swim,' he reminded her, picturing her in a very small bikini, emerging from waves. It was a very distracting image. 'Well, this is your suite.' He tipped his head and walked away. 'Half an hour, then.'

She wanted to ask where he was sleeping but stopped herself. It sounded too needy. She thought of saying she wasn't hungry but she realised she was actually starving. Nerves had meant she hadn't eaten a thing all day.

Kat walked in the room and leaned against the door. The room she had entered was furnished in the style of a French chateau, the walls peachy gold in colour, the stunning fireplace with its top-heavy carving dominating the room.

She found the opulent luxuriousness of it all fascinating. The antiques, the drapes, the handmade wallpaper. This was the embodiment of money being no object. It was clear there had been an effort made to inject some personal touches. Kat was appreciative of the flowers and candles. The antique furniture, probably worth a fortune, was all a bit too ornate to ever feel comfortable; her tastes were simpler.

The bathroom was a place where she didn't mind the extravagance. It was spectacular. Someone had already lit the candles around the massive copper tub. She was sorely tempted but was conscious of the time factor and Zach's parting words. Instead, she contented herself with washing her face—her make-up was long gone anyway. She applied a smudge of grey shadow to her eyelids, two flicks of mascara, and rubbed some clear gold on her lips. Her hair, after a severe brush, she left shiny and loose, before changing her top for a clean, though slightly creased, black silk blouse from her case, which somehow had arrived in the room before her.

With three minutes to spare she was outside the bedroom in the corridor, not pausing to analyse her determination not to have him step inside her room. It wasn't as if he was going to carry her through to the French-boudoir bedroom with its canopied bed that was probably a lot of women's dream. The same women probably dreamt of having a man like Zach throw them on it and make mad, passionate, head-banging love to them…or should that be *with* them?

She had never felt that her ignorance of head-banging sex was a disadvantage in life previously, but now she found herself wondering what she was missing.

'You don't want to know, Kat. It's not you.'

The echo of her announcement had barely died away before a voice very close by responded.

'What don't you want to know?'

Kat felt as if guilt was written all over her face, but she managed a very credible recovery. 'If they dress for dinner here.' It was, she decided, inspirational but, now that she thought about it, actually quite relevant.

'Well, there is no *they*, just us, and as you see…'

She accepted the invitation of his downward sweeping gesture and felt her tummy muscles quiver in helpless appreciation as she took in the pale shirt, open at the neck, and the black jeans that clung to his narrow hips and suggested the powerful musculature of his thighs.

The wash of colour lent a peachy glow to her skin as she put effort into controlling her breathing and dragged her eyes back to his face. His dark hair was damp, as though he'd just stepped out of the shower.

'That's good, then.' She turned and began to walk briskly away. He let her go a few feet before calling after her.

'Wrong direction.'

She compressed her lips. 'You might have said!'

He might have, but the truth was he had been enjoying her rear view too much. 'Sorry.'

'I'm not really a formal sort of person.'

'Alekis rarely entertains, but I'm sure he will want to show you off when he is discharged.'

She turned her head, falling into step beside him. 'He looked…frail. How ill is he, really?'

'He has a history of what I believe he euphemistically has in the past called "cardiac events". This time, however, he had more than one cardiac arrest. He is not a young man.'

'You mean he died?' His neutral delivery made it impossible for her to figure out if he would care one way or the other. She got it that some people didn't wear their heart on their sleeve, but this was ridiculous!

Did he think it was weakness to show emotion?

'So they tell me.'

'Should I…?' She shook her head. 'No, it doesn't matter—'

He hefted a sigh. 'Your first lesson is to stop thinking about what the right thing is, and think instead about what you want.'

She skipped a little to catch him up and angled a puzzled look at his profile. 'Do you mean you *never* do anything you don't really want to?'

'Why would I?' It was a question he had been trying to answer since Alekis had foisted the task of bringing his granddaughter home. A spreadsheet would have shown that any debt he felt towards Alekis was fully paid up by the knife he'd taken for him, but some things could not be defined by spreadsheets and analysis.

His instinct, honed by his visceral hatred of bullies, had saved Alekis's life, but Alekis had enabled him to rewrite his own life. He would always owe Alekis. It was not something that he could analyse, it was just something he accepted.

His eyes drifted to the cloud of dark hair, loosened now, that fell almost all the way down to her narrow waist. His acceptance meant he would never feel that silky hair slide through his fingers.

'Oh, I don't know, because it's the right thing?'

He dug his hands deep in his pockets. 'Who decides what the right thing is? But the answer is, no, I don't. You are looking at me as though you have just discovered a different species. I promise you, Katina, I am not the one that is different.'

'You make it sound like it's a bad thing to be different.'

'When different involves you believing in the Easter Bunny, Santa Claus and the basic goodness of your fellow man after the age of nine, then, yes, it is a bad thing, a very bad thing. I believe we are eating in here.' He paused outside an open doorway and gestured for her to precede him.

'You are the most cynical man I have ever met.' She paused on the threshold. 'Oh, this is pretty,' she exclaimed as she registered the table set before the open French doors. Light, gauzy window coverings were fluttering in the light sea breeze that caused the lit candles to flicker and dance. 'I thought all the rooms were massive here.'

'I thought, after the day you have had, you might like something slightly less...formal?' He had phoned ahead to ask for the staff presence to be kept to a minimum to give her some breathing space.

Her eyes flew to his face, then, aware that her pleasure at the small consideration was excessive, she turned and walked across to the open doors to breathe in the fragrance blowing in from the water.

'I can hear the sea!'

'Hard to escape it. We are on an island.'

She swivelled around to face him. 'Well, I have never lived on a private island so I can't be quite so bored about it as you.'

What amazed him was she appeared utterly oblivious to the fact that, standing there with the moonlit, star-studded sky as backdrop, the spider's-web-fine curtains blowing around her face like a bride's veil, she looked utterly beautiful.

In this era of air-brushed perfection, she stood out, not just for her natural beauty, but her total lack of artifice. The inner sexuality that she was totally oblivious of added another transfixing layer to her appeal.

The idea of enjoying that sensuality, of wrapping himself in it, and her hair, raised his core temperature several degrees, which made him a little more effusive than he might normally have been when Selene arrived before he could say something really stupid, like, *Let's skip the food and go to bed*.

'Wow, multitasking tonight, Selene? Isn't this a bit below your pay grade?'

Mouth prim, but smiling with her eyes, the housekeeper gestured to the two maids in uniform who appeared, pushing a trolley on wheels.

'I have followed your instructions. It will be informal, but I wanted to see personally that Kat is comfortable.' She nodded to the girls and said something in Greek that prompted them both to busy themselves with the items on the trolley.

Kat approached the chair that Zach held, nodding a silent thank you as she took her seat. 'I'm very comfortable, thank you,' she said, thinking it was *almost* true now she couldn't feel the warmth of his breath on her cheek, just the tingle it had left behind. There were disadvantages to the sense of intimacy this room gave.

The housekeeper lifted the lids from the dishes on the trolley, inspecting each one before she nodded and turned back to the diners. 'Eloise…just put it down.' The young maid nodded and put a dessert she carried onto the serving table.

'Right, I'll leave you to open the wine, shall I?'
She looked at Zach and at the champagne cooling
in a cut-glass bucket.

'So does he…my grandfather eat here when
he's alone?'

Selene gave a choke that might have been laughter before she whisked from the room.

'Did I say something wrong?'

His sensual lips quirked into a half-smile. 'Actually, Alekis eats in the main dining room, which
is the size of a football pitch, and he would find
it strange if he had to pour his own wine…or, for
that matter, water.'

'So this is?'

'This is a private dining room used exclusively
when your grandfather is entertaining one of his…
friends.'

For a moment she looked blank, then comprehension dawned. 'He has…' Her eyes widened
some more. 'But he's *old*!'

Zach's lips twitched. 'Not *too* old, apparently.'
He leaned back in his seat and looked at her. 'So
is any of this what you were expecting?'

'I'm not sure what I was expecting. Mum used
to tell me that one day I'd have beautiful dresses,
and I have.' She had found a wardrobe the size of
her flat in London crammed with designer labels.
A small smile played across her soft lips as her
wistful gaze drifted to the fluttering candles on

the table. 'A birthday cake with lots of candles. Apart from the birthday bit, it's all here.'

'Do you like seafood?'

She jumped a little, jolting away the memories that curved her lips into a soft smile. 'I like everything,' she said honestly. 'But I'm allergic to nuts.'

Zach could tell by her expression that another memory had been triggered—he didn't want to ask, didn't want to find himself rediscovering how uncomfortable empathy was. It was masochistic, but somehow, he couldn't stop himself.

'What are you thinking about?'

Her eyes fell from his as he walked with his own plate back to his seat. 'This looks delicious.' She looked up from her plate and their glances connected. 'When Mum… When the police went to the flat.'

Kat could remember but hadn't understood at the time the glances the policewomen had exchanged when she'd given her name and address. Though pretty gentrified now, at that time it was not a *nice* area.

'She had left a note. I have it. I had access to my files after I decided to look for her,' she explained. The decision had not been made lightly. She'd known there were risks, most importantly the risk of being rejected all over again. 'I thought she might have another family and I might be a reminder of a past she wanted to forget.'

'You went ahead anyway.' They had both re-traced their pasts, but with very different aims. He had wanted closure and, if he was honest, to rub his success in their faces, show them what he had achieved despite them. And she, as far as he could tell, had simply wanted to reconnect, to sat-isfy her craving for family.

She had forgiven, he never would. This would always set them apart.

She gave a little shrug. 'It took longer than I thought. She seemed to have dropped off the grid after she...left. It never even occurred to me that she might be...not alive.'

He watched as she lowered her eyes so he couldn't see the tears and waited as she speared a prawn onto her fork and slowly chewed it, curs-ing himself for asking for an answer that he knew was going to make him feel emotions that had no purpose, and yet he was being controlled by something stronger than logic—a primal need to protect.

He might have been able to fight his reaction to her beauty, but when that beauty came attached to a vulnerability not masked by her air of indepen-dent fighting spirit, it awoke something in him that he had never felt before. He didn't want to feel it.

'The note she left said...' Kat stared at her plate as she began to recite, '"He made me choose, and Katina is a good girl, and I'm no good for her anyway. PS: She's allergic to nuts.'" Her flat delivery did not disguise the fact that reciting the words hurt her.

The fingers around his heart tightened as she lifted her head and said defiantly, 'She wanted me to be safe.'

If she ever had a child, Kat thought, he or she would *know* they were safe. She would never leave them, not for a man, not for *anything*.

Zach bit back the retort on his tongue. Maybe she *needed* to think that her mother had cared about her. What did he know? Maybe the woman had. Why was he worrying one way or the other? he asked himself, resenting how she had intruded into the emotional isolation. Yet when he looked at her, he couldn't be angry. He felt empathy; like a limb deprived of blood flow, the reawakening of this dormant emotion was painful.

'And were you?'

Deliberately misunderstanding him, she grinned and patted a pocket. 'I always carry my EpiPen just in case.' She speared another prawn. 'This is delicious.'

'I'll let the kitchens know about the nut allergy.'

'Don't worry, if in doubt I don't eat it. The allergy is not as serious as some. I know someone who went into anaphylactic shock because she kissed her boyfriend and he'd just eaten a curry with nuts in.'

'So your boyfriends have to swear off nuts?'

The way he was looking at her mouth made the heat climb into her cheeks, and other places. She shifted uneasily in her seat. 'I'm not that bad.' She pushed aside her plate and took a sip of the champagne. It seemed a good time to change the subject. 'So it sounds like Selene has known you for a long time.'

He arched a satiric brow. 'You mean she doesn't treat me with sufficient deference.'

The fact that he could mock himself was a pleasant surprise.

'I was quite young when I first visited the island.'

It frequently seemed to him that Selene still saw him as the young truculent teen with a massive chip on his shoulder and on more than one occasion the family silver in his pockets. His convalescence had been eventful for the new housekeeper, as Selene had been back then.

Kat, trying to imagine what young Zach had looked like, wondered if Selene had some photos of him too. She laid her napkin down on her side plate and decided against another sip of the fizz. The first had gone to her head after the long day. Her appetite after the first few bites had vanished too. She lifted a hand to hide a yawn.

'You're tired.' Of course she was—how could she not be after the day she'd had? He felt the painful twisting sensation in his chest as he watched her stifle another yawn, realising she'd been running on adrenaline all evening.

She shook her head. 'No, not really.'

'You are,' he said, laying down his napkin. 'You need your rest. Tomorrow is another long day. We'll go over the guest list in the morning.' The morning made him think of the night that preceded it. Waking up together, her head on his chest, their limbs tangled. *Tangled*—the word jolted him free of the images flickering through his head.

He did not do *tangled*—emotionally or in any other way. He liked clean-cut defined lines, minus entanglements, which were far more likely to occur if a man spent the entire night in a woman's bed. *Any* woman, let alone the granddaughter of his mentor!

Her brows twitched. 'Guest list?'

'I've compiled a who's who list of the guests for tomorrow along with a bio.'

Her eyes widened. 'Is there an exam…?'

Her comment wrenched a bark of deep laughter from his throat. Then, as their eyes connected, dark on amber, the amusement faded first from his, and then hers.

The air suddenly crackled with a sensually charged tension that seemed to suck the oxygen from the atmosphere, drawing them deeper into a sensual vortex that swirled around them.

Light-headed, Kat didn't connect the sound she could hear with her own laboured breathing, her heart thudding like a dull metronome in her chest as she experienced a surge of deep, strength-sapping longing.

Zach watched the pupils in her eyes expand until only a rim of gold remained. He could hear the roar of hunger in his blood and wanted… *Theos*, how *badly* he wanted to give himself up to it, sink into her softness and… The muscles in his brown throat rippled as he swallowed and dug deep into the reserves of his frayed self-control.

Kat blinked, confused as Zach suddenly surged to his feet, not quite meeting her eyes as he bent forward, the flickering candlelight throwing the planes and angles of his face into stark relief as he blew out the candles.

The gesture seemed weirdly symbolic to Kat because, along with the candlelight, the intimacy had vanished. Been snuffed out, to be replaced by a cool, businesslike atmosphere as he walked towards the door, having donned the persona of the ruthless tycoon with computer chips, not emotions, in his eyes.

'I'll get someone to walk you back to your room.'

She blinked, getting to her feet in confusion as his mercurial mood change made her head spin. 'Aren't you—?'

His quick smile was impersonal and distant. It

seemed to her he couldn't get out of the door fast enough. 'I have some work to get through.'

In the corridor, Zach propped his broad shoulders against the wall and released a long, slow, sibilant sigh. It was not pride enhancing to realise that the only effective way he had been able to see to remove himself from temptation was to remove himself physically.

He levered himself off the wall, aware that if he had escorted her back to her room he might have ended up saying good morning and not goodnight. Even the thought of it now heated his blood in a way that drew a low snarling sound from his throat as he strode off, putting as much distance as possible between himself and the witch who had put a spell on him.

CHAPTER EIGHT

THE PLACE BOASTED a state-of-the-art gym that Zach doubted Alekis even knew existed, but he chose the beach ahead of the treadmill. Two hours of flat-out pushing-himself-to-the-limit running later, he felt he had regained a sense of proportion, enabling him to think past crippling lust and recognise that being thrown into the company of someone whose early life mirrored his own to some minor degree had dredged up some deeply buried memories, and added an intensity to his feelings when she was around.

A logical explanation, without falling back on the tired old clichés of soul mates, made him feel more comfortable and confident he was able to deal with the next few days without betraying Alekis's trust.

He just needed to keep her at an emotional arm's length and fulfil his commitment to Alekis.

Having breakfasted alone, Kat asked directions to the study, where apparently Zach was waiting for her.

The question in her mind was, *which* Zach?

It seemed to Kat that there were more than one. There was the Zach who seemed warm and interested, even sympathetic, when she told him about her past, or the one who was the distant and cool executive hiding behind defensive walls to keep emotions out.

She understood the decision to protect her heart in an emotional armour, but her heart had always ached for people who didn't realise they had imprisoned themselves at the same time. *Not your business, Kat,* she told herself firmly.

The thought had been a recurring theme through the long night that had been punctuated by fitful dreams, a session of trying on shoes from the cavernous wardrobe and minutes spent on the balcony, listening to the soothing sound of the waves.

Thank God for caffeine!

'Good morning, did you sleep well? Excellent.'

She blinked. So this was how it was going to be?

'Coffee?' He stood there with pot in hand, more good-looking than any man had a right to be in a black T-shirt and jeans. If his manner had been as informal as his clothes, she'd have been toast. It wasn't, so she wasn't. All positive—this was not the right time to develop a crush and this was not the Zach whose opinion she would ask about the outfit she had chosen for this evening.

'Yes, please, black.' Matching his manner, she

took a sip of the scalding strong brew, though the effort was wasted on him as he'd already turned to the desk. 'Right, there will be thirty-five guests tonight. I have subdivided them—society, business and social.' He stabbed a long finger towards the screen of the tablet that was on the desk and tagged on casually, 'Only one royal.'

'Only one?'

He flashed her a look. 'He won't be a problem,' he promised, dismissing blue blood with a snap of his long fingers. 'However, these might. You can see…'

She couldn't. She was still standing on the other side of the room. Seeing his look of impatience, she overcame her reluctance to move closer, and after a moment's hesitation she reacted to his gesture to step in and look, planting her hands palms flat on the surface as she leaned in.

'As you can see, I have red-flagged those who might be a problem,' he explained. 'Number one is probably Spiro Alekides.' He leaned across her, causing her breath to hitch as he scrolled down the screen before moving back to a distance she found comfortable once more as he explained, 'He can be slippery and has an unsavoury reputation when it comes to women.'

Kat turned her head. He had said that with no discernible trace of irony in his voice, and, yes,

there was none at all on his face that she could see—
staggering!

'Unfortunately, Alekis has a joint venture with
him,' he tagged on, explaining the man's presence.

'You don't sound as though you approve?'

'Alekis does not need my approval.'

'Who is she?' Kat asked, looking curiously at
the glamorous blonde woman whose photo was
next to the red-flagged man.

'That's Ariana.'

Something in his voice made her turn again
in response to a little spurt of something alarm-
ingly close to jealousy tightening in her chest. 'You
know her?'

'That sort of intuition will do you no harm,' he
complimented her smoothly. 'We have both dated
Ariana, as it happens at the same time. Spiro sent
her to do a little industrial espionage and I used
the situation to my advantage to plant a little false
information. He has never actually forgiven me,
so keep clear,' he warned.

Kat caught her breath. This was not *close* to
jealousy, and more a flood than a spurt. This was
the real thing with bells on! The shaft that pierced
her was so intense that she would not have been
surprised to see a knife hilt protruding from her
chest.

Kat was as deeply shocked by her visceral reaction as she was scared by it. Lowering her gaze

to hide the emotions she felt were written across her face in neon letters, she amazed herself by responding in a relatively calm voice.

'So she used you, and you used her. Does that cancel out all the using?' she wondered in a voice that sounded too bright. 'I'll look at this myself later. Don't worry, I always did my homework.'

Aware that Zach was watching her with a puzzled frown, she struggled to control her expression and presumably failed; she could hear the suspicion in his voice as he asked, 'What's wrong?'

'Not a thing.' She tucked the tablet under her arm. 'I promised myself I'd explore this morning.'

'Want a guide?'

'I think I'll be fine on my own.' She had to get out of the room before he guessed, which would be the ultimate humiliation!

He stared at the door, fighting the impulse that gripped him to follow her before he slumped down into one of the chairs. It was time to stop pretending and face facts. When it came to this woman his normal iron control did not apply.

More by luck than good judgement, she found her way back to her suite. Nobody had cleared the shoes that had littered the bedroom floor since she had pulled them out of the cavernous closet in the early hours of the morning. She kicked one of the soft-as-butter lemon-coloured pumps that were lovely, almost tripped over the striking red loafers, and picked up one of the cute kitten heels in one hand, and one of the spiky, far too high ankle boots, sexy as hell—even with pyjamas— in the other.

With a low moan, she threw them both across the room, then, feeling guilty that she was leaving someone else to pick them up, gathered up the shoes and, pairing them all up, stacked them neatly in their boxes, telling herself that she needed to get a grip. She needed to focus and *not* think about Zach Garros.

She spent the next hour lying, head propped in her hands, on the bed, poring over the guest list and the cream of Athens society. But for some reason it wasn't sinking in, so she welcomed the interruption when a maid tapped on the door.

'Mrs Carras asks me to tell you that there is morning tea in the small salon if you wish it, miss?'

Why not? thought Kat, closing the tablet.

'Lead the way,' she said to the girl, who looked startled by the informality.

An hour later, as she sipped her second cup of tea, Kat walked to the high, deep windows. The sea shone in the near distance like silvered turquoise in the morning sun. As the place was built on a peninsula projecting into the water, she assumed that most rooms would have similarly breathtaking marine vistas.

Selene bustled in. Kat found herself envying the woman's vaguely harassed air and realised she was bored. She was used to being busy. She would make a very poor lady of leisure.

'Good morning. Did you sleep well?'

'Perfectly,' Kat lied. 'I thought I might explore a little this morning, if there's nothing you want me—?' she began hopefully.

'Gracious, no. I'll send Della. She can be your guide and she's too teary this morning to be any help—she's in love,' Selene added with an eye-roll.

'No, don't worry. I'd prefer to wander alone, if that's okay?'

'Of course. Enjoy yourself.'

A little exploration had proved her assumption was right: the scale of the building was daunting and then some. She hesitated to call it a home. It seemed more to her like a massive status symbol. *Surely* no one needed this much space?

She got turned around several times during her exploration until she realised that the place was built on a grid system. After that her attempts to get her bearings got a little easier. Everything fanned out from one central living area. She supposed that you got your head around massive in time—less so the presence of staff, discreet but liable to pop up and take you by surprise. She hoped some of them were temporary additions for the evening event.

It was her first test and one she hadn't decided if she actually wanted to pass. Who was she trying to please and impress? The grandfather she didn't know, or the man who didn't care one way or the other?

Maybe, Kat, you should try pleasing yourself?

It was a plan.

The first of the two wings she explored seemed to be dedicated to private suites, like her own, and some slightly smaller guest suites. After half an hour of opening doors and admiring views she wandered back out to the terrace that ran the full length of this side of the building. Beautifully manicured lawns ran down to the sea. She took off her cardigan. It felt like spring as she took a seat on one of the long stone benches surrounded by tubs of flowers. Selene appeared, along with a young girl in a maid's uniform who she introduced as Della.

The appearance was so perfectly timed that Kat imagined her every move being picked up by CCTV cameras. She smiled at the girl, recognising the name, but didn't get a smile back, just a quick curtsey and a look that mingled tragic with sulky. She was not a recommendation for love with the black mascara rings around her eyes.

Selene noticed this, too. 'Go on, run along and wash your face,' she said, and the girl rushed off.

'It's such beautiful weather here, I can't get over it.' She had as little control over that as she did her visceral response to Zach, but the weather was much easier to live with.

'Yes, and such a relief after the heat. The summer was hot even for here. You are finding your way around?'

Kat's smile was a poor disguise for the fact she was overwhelmed by everything. She fought her way through a wave of longing for the comfortable predictability of her old life and nodded. 'There is a lot to explore.'

'Are you sure you don't want someone to show you around? Not Della,' she added hastily. 'That girl is just… She is really trying my patience today.'

'Actually, it's quite nice discovering things on my own, and if I have a guide to rely on it will take me for ever to find my way around.'

The older woman nodded and smiled. 'Oh, I should mention that the room is being prepared for this evening, so there might be a little disruption. Can I get you anything—tea, coffee, cakes?'

'Tea would be nice,' she lied, thinking, *This is how bored people put on weight.* 'So, I'm assuming the guests will be staying overnight?' It wasn't as if there weren't room.

'Normally they would, but, no, Mr Zach has arranged transport. They will be leaving by eight-thirty sharp.' Kat picked up on the 'whether they like it or not' silent addition. 'Hence the early start this evening. If you'll excuse me, the musicians have arrived and they are being a little…artistic.' She rolled her eyes and whisked away.

When the tea arrived it came with some delicious little honey pastries embedded with nuts and jewelled candy fruit, which Kat, who told herself she was still making up for her half-eaten dinner, demolished.

Exploring the second wing didn't really work off many calories, Kat discovered. It was dedicated to the domestic area. Her appearance in a food-preparation room created a bit of a shock panic moment for the staff working there.

She apologised and backed out, then promptly lost her orientation once more and ended up outside again where she discovered that there was more than one swimming pool, and this one was in an enclosed courtyard. A shaded area lay to one side of the marble-floored space complete with what appeared to be an outdoor kitchen; on a raised plinth on the opposite side, a massive spa pool bubbled away happily.

She lay down on one of the loungers with a bump, marvelling at how different this world was compared to the one she was used to.

Not my world, but I'm still me.

The recognition eased the tightness in her chest. Her chin lifted. If she was going to do this, she'd do it her way. For starters, she'd do what she always did. Focus not on the negative but the positive. Yes, heiress was a bad fit for her, but she'd worn ill-fitting shoes before now and survived, she reminded herself, and they'd always looked good.

She'd already saved the refuge... If she was going to inherit money and power, there were a lot of worthy causes out there who just needed someone to notice them.

When a menu appeared for her lunch, Kat requested a sandwich. She intended to explore the gardens and beach.

'Just a sandwich?' Della looked confused. 'What will I tell Mrs Carras?'

'That I want a sandwich.'

Her irritation fell away as, without warning, the young girl's face suddenly crumpled and she burst into loud sobs.

'Fine, I'll have lunch,' Kat said, alarmed. The girl continued to sob.

'*He's* sending him away and I'll never see him again, and I love him!'

'Take a seat.' She got up and the girl took her own, scrubbing her face with her apron. 'Della, is it...? Who is *he*? The first *he*.'

'Mr Gavros. Alexi thinks he's marvellous, but

he's not—he's cruel and heartless and he's sending Alexi away because he thinks I'm too young!
And he doesn't want anyone to be happy!'

Kat had never been so glad to see anyone as
she was to see Selene. The older woman took one
look at the scene and bustled the weeping girl out.
A few moments later she returned.

'I am so sorry about that.'

'It's fine. She says that Zach is sending her boyfriend away.'

'Oh, I know. She's telling anyone who will listen the same thing.'

While Kat was the first to believe that Zach
was no saint, that he was cynical and manipulative, the girl's story just didn't have a ring of truth
to it. Why on earth would Zach go out of his way
to blight young love? Mock it, yes, but not… No,
she was sure there was another explanation.

'So, is he?'

The other woman gave a chuckle. 'Well, I suppose he is. Alexi is one of the placements, one of
the big successes, and, as you might know, Zach
has an arrangement with the university: if the
youngsters he recommends pass the interview and
entrance exam they are admitted without formal
exams to do a foundation year. Alexi is starting
next semester. The boy, as bright as they come, is
over the moon.'

Kat tried to pick her way through the information. 'So, this Alexi was originally—?'

'Much like Zach, living on the streets, though obviously his situation was not as dire as Zach's.' The older woman, unaware she had just dropped a bombshell, shook her head while Kat's imagination went into riot mode. 'Not all the youngsters end up in academia, obviously, but they are all offered a way out, a safe way out.'

Kat shook her head. Zach had lived on the streets? She knew his family situation had been bad...*outsider*, he'd said. Now she fully understood what he had meant.

'So, he escaped his family by living on the streets.' The ache in the little corner of her heart was not just for the boy he had once been, but the lone wolf he had become.

Presumably it had been her grandfather who had taken him out of that old life, which perhaps explained the loyalty he seemed to feel towards the older man.

She gave a sudden laugh as she realised that, ironically, it turned out that Zach was as much of a member of the *do-gooding* fraternity he claimed to despise as she was!

Happily, Selene misinterpreted her amusement.

'I know, young love. The thing is,' she said, lowering her voice to a confidential whisper, 'I think young Alexi is quite relieved. Della is a rather *in-*

tense girl and very young for her age.' She hefted out a sigh. 'Better to give her the day off than risk any more meltdowns, I think. I'll leave you to your exploring.'

Her exploring took Kat to the beach, where she peeled off the clothes over the black swimsuit she'd put on earlier. She could not swim but she could paddle. She waded out, thigh deep, staring, eyes scrunched against the sun, out to sea. She let her thoughts drift—the tide took them inevitably in the direction of Zach. Would she challenge him with his background, ask him why he was so afraid anyone might suspect he was a good guy?

It was almost as if he had tried to make her think the worst of him earlier. Maybe there was a worse but there was also a *better*. A better he seemed not to want anyone to see…*or is that just me?*

She shook her head as she collapsed onto the warm sand. The man was a confusing mass of contradictions! As she shook back her hair she let the sun dry the moisture from her skin, rubbing the sand away as it dried on her bare arms and legs.

It was only when she removed her watch from the pocket where she had put it for safekeeping that she noticed the time. With a yelp, she jumped to her feet, dragged her clothes on over her now dry swimsuit and began to jog up the deserted beach.

She had reached the green manicured lawns that

ran down to the sand when she collided not with one of the palms, but a solidity that had warmth.

If his hands had not remained on her shoulders she would have fallen over. Her hands clutched his hair-roughened, sinewy forearms as she inhaled a deep breath of his warm male scent, causing her stomach to violently clench in hopeless desire.

Slowly, her eyes lifted, over the clinging T-shirt stretched across his broad chest to his face. Like the rest of his skin, it was filmed with salty moisture.

She didn't say a word; she couldn't. She ached for him. Quite literally. She hadn't thought it was possible.

It took every ounce of his willpower to resist the longing in her eyes as she looked up at him. Alekis's granddaughter who needed...*deserved* more than someone like him could give.

'You don't look in the party mood.' Hair wild, skin glazed with a sun-kissed look, her lips lightly crusted with salt that he longed to kiss off, she looked the ultimate in desirability.

Kat swallowed the occlusion in her throat; her chest felt constricted and tight. He was close, *too* close. She couldn't breathe, or think, just feel. Too much feeling.

'I'm in panic mode. I'm cutting it a bit fine, probably.' She lifted a hand to her tangled hair and took a step back. His hands fell away as she looked at him through her lashes.

'I should run,' she said, thinking, *Don't let me.*

'Yes.'

She was still running as she entered her suite, brought to a panting, shocked immobility by what waited for her there.

'Good evening,' she said pleasantly to the small army of assorted people assembled inside her private salon. *What the hell?*

She looked to Selene, brows raised, for explanation, even though the hairdryers, tongs and assorted brushes sticking out of a couple of bags was a clue.

'I thought you might like to start getting ready now?' Selene's anxious glance at the ormolu clock over the fireplace that held a massive flower arrangement suggested that she thought this process should have begun some time earlier, and, considering Kat's salty hair had taken on a life of its own, she couldn't really blame her.

'Oh, have you been waiting?'

'Not at all,' came the polite lie.

'Actually, you can all have the evening off,' she said, addressing the small makeover army. 'I'm more than happy to get myself ready.'

The expression of shock and consternation on the older woman's face almost made Kat smile.

Clearly the idea that Kat could dress herself, do her own hair and apply her make-up shocked the present company deeply. They *wanted* to argue, Kat could *feel* it.

'Honestly, I've been dressing myself for years.'

Nobody smiled. Kat felt her impatience edge up; she enjoyed a spa day as much as anyone, but she couldn't see it becoming part of her daily routine, or even *big* day routine.

She'd read about freak shows and she supposed this was the modern version—she being the freak!

Damping down her mounting panic, she tried again. 'Honestly, I'll be fine, but if I have a problem I'll yell.'

She utilised a smile aimed at robbing her refusal of any offence and firmly closed her bedroom door on their collective shocked faces. It took her a moment to find the music selection she was looking for and turn up the volume. It wasn't as if there were any neighbours to worry about.

One of these days she was going to take up yoga, but in the meantime her tried-and-tested relaxation method of choice was what it always had been—a five-minute session of wild, unrestrained, let-your-hair-down dancing to a rock anthem while quite frequently singing along.

When the track came to an end, she switched the music off and fell back headlong onto the canopied bed. Staring at the ceiling, she waited for her heart rate to slow to a gentle trot.

To say she was relaxed would have been an exaggeration, but she was willing to accept exhaustion as a substitute—she was just too tired to run away. The thought brought an image of her running away from Zach on the beach. She had stopped once and he'd still been standing there staring after her. The image in her head made her stomach flip.

'Oh, God, this is crazy!' she groaned as she padded to the bathroom. Sadly, she hadn't left herself enough time for a long and lazy bath. The deep double-ended copper tub that took centre stage in the bathroom…now that was one luxury item she might get used to quite quickly.

Sniffing some of the lovely oils lined up, she stripped and walked into the shower, which was big enough to house a football team, though the image that slid into her head did not involve a team, just one man…who was constantly on her mind!

But not your bed, Kat, mocked the voice in her head.

It was about time she remembered she was not the sort of woman who undressed men, even in her imagination, let alone… She scrunched her face and threw a mental bucket of cold water over the febrile images.

Wrapped in a towel, duly anointed with some delicious moisturising lotion, her hair clear of salt, the last traces of sand washed from the crevices it had crawled into, she looked at the dress she had finally selected in the early hours from the racks in the massive walk-in closet.

It was midnight blue, so dark it looked black in certain lights—basically it was a slim ankle-length slip, not that there was anything *basic* about the cut of the heavy silk, high at the neck and low enough at the back to expose her delicately sculptured shoulder blades.

After blast-drying her long thick hair, she tried a couple of styles, almost wishing she had not rejected the services of a hairstylist, and then as she pulled her thick glossy skeins into a knot on the nape of her neck things clicked. She smoothed it properly and gathered it again, winding the sections into a smooth loose knot at the nape of her neck before sticking in several hairpins to secure it, then finally pulling out a few face-framing strands for a softening effect.

Her normal make-up was a smudge of shadow, a touch of gloss on her lips. So the fifteen minutes she did spend felt like a long time, but the end result, if not perfect, satisfied her. The dusting of blush on her cheeks lifted her pallor and the highlighter along her cheekbones worked. She carefully highlighted the almond shape of her eyes with liner before adding a sweep of mascara over her already dark and lustrous eyelashes.

She struggled to adjust the narrow straps of the dress so that they left the delicate architecture of her collarbones exposed, before slipping into the heels. She was viewing the overall effect with a critical eye when there was a knock on the door, a polite reminder from Selene.

She took a deep breath and straightened her shoulders. She couldn't pretend this wasn't really going to happen any longer, but she could pretend her stomach wasn't churning in apprehension.

Smile in place, projecting a confidence she was far from feeling, she pulled the door open. Her smile wilted and died like a rose exposed to an icy chill. A myriad sensations and emotions that were impossible to detangle hit her simultaneously as she saw the tall figure, no longer in running shorts and vest, but in the dress suit, dark hair still visibly damp as though he had just stepped from a shower. An image that did not help her composure, or her heart, which literally stalled. For several moments she felt as if it would never start again.

'You scared the life out of me!' Breathless, and sounding it, she lifted a hand to her throat, where she could feel a pulse that was trying to fight its way through her skin.

Zach cleared his own throat. It had been less a jolt and more an earth tremor to see her standing there and for several heartbeats he'd stood, literally transfixed.

'I really didn't think you scared that easily.'

She was the most fearless woman he had ever met and—as he looked at her standing there now, there was no use pretending otherwise—the most beautiful.

Against the dark fabric her skin gleamed pale gold. Her body, under the figure-enhancing cut of the midnight fabric, was slender and sensuous. The way she wore her hair displayed the length of her slender neck and her delicate collarbones. She looked exclusive and sexy—a hard look to pull off.

He leaned a hand on the doorjamb above her head. 'If you are dressing to impress you have succeeded. You look very lovely.'

Her breath caught at the compliment.

'I wanted to blend in,' she said in a small husky voice, worrying that he might assume she had made the effort to impress him. Worried even more because she couldn't swear she hadn't!

It was hard to smile with the ache in his groin, but he did anyway. 'Ah, well, you failed.' Straightening up, he gestured to her to walk beside him and after a short pause she did, her perfume making his nostrils flare.

'How was your run?'

He flashed her a frowning look. *'Hot.'*

'When is Alekis's surgery scheduled for?'

'First thing Thursday if the rest of the tests are clear.'

'Should I go there to see him before?'

'If you want to.'

'Is the surgery dangerous?'

'Another bypass and a valve replacement, I believe.'

It was weird but hearing all this life-and-death stuff suddenly made the lies she'd been telling herself all day seem petty and ridiculous.

For someone who had spent her life avoiding excitement and danger, it was not easy to acknowledge the idea that had been growing in her head. Because if danger had a name and a face and a really incredible body, she was thinking of throwing herself at him, *giving* herself to him. The thought was scary and liberating at the same time.

Zach just tapped into a reckless part of her. It had required no effort on his part; just breathing did it. Her response would require more effort. Forget instincts, she needed to use her brain.

It would have been helpful if he had remained the unacceptable but very handsome face of capitalism; instead, she knew more, knew there was nothing two-dimensional about him. She understood when people did not want to discuss their backgrounds for fear of others assuming they were using it in some way, but why hide the things he was giving back to society?

She took a shallow breath and closed down the conflicting theories whirring around in her head. She had to get through the next couple of hours first.

'Well?'

He arched a brow. 'Well, what?' And carried on walking, requiring her to skip on her heels to catch him up.

'Well, isn't there a list? Don't eat with your mouth full, don't get drunk and dance on the tables, don't talk politics, insult the guests or slag off the powerful and influential even if they are total sleazes?'

'I think you have covered the essentials and the file had everything you need in it.' He paused. 'But actually no one here should give you a hard time. This *will* get easier.'

'Well, at least I won't get drunk so there will be no online pictures of me dancing on the table. I only got drunk once and I didn't like it.' The memory made her wince, but underneath she was feeling moderately pleased she was proving they could have a normal conversation without any sex stuff getting in the way. *It had all been in her head anyway.*

He looked amused. 'It rarely stops anyone repeating the process.'

'I had my drink spiked.'

The amusement slid from his eyes. She had the

impression he didn't even know that he put his
hands heavily on her shoulders, but she knew they
felt very heavy; she couldn't move.

Actually, she wasn't really trying.

'What happened?'

'I was at a nightclub for someone's birthday. It
was all right, my friends got me out of there.' She
chose not to think what might have happened if
they hadn't, if the two men trying to half-carry
her out to the waiting car had succeeded. 'For a
while I struggled with trust, but then I realised I
was letting fear rule my life.' She stepped a little
ahead of him, paused and twirled around to face
him, hitting him full blast with her golden stare,
leaving him no escape route.

'You have to trust someone sometime, don't you
think, Zach?'

He could feel the pulse pounding in his temple.
'Is there some sort of message in there for me?'

She shrugged. 'Just throwing it out there. Some
people are bad. They hurt you, but there are a lot
of people that are good, too. You miss such a lot
by pushing them away.'

'And if someone spikes your drink?'

'I refuse to live in fear…' Her beautiful smile
flashed out. 'I had friends to look out for me and
here… I have you, *I think*?'

He ignored the voice in his head that yelled
coward, his eyes sliding from hers. 'Tonight you

do, but there are a lot of tomorrows. There is such a thing as too trusting, Katina.'

'How so?'

The exhaustion came over him in a tide; fighting the uncontrollable urge to take her in his arms became in the space of a heartbeat just too much. He stopped fighting and surrendered to the roar and the hunger, the ache of wanting.

Holding her wide eyes with his, he placed one large hand in the small of her back, noting the flare in her golden eyes as he curved his free hand around the back of her head and dragged her into him.

She did register that the combustible, exciting quality that she was always conscious of in him was not in the background but right there, in her face, reminding her he was too male, too *everything*. But nothing running through her head had prepared her for what his intention was. She was in denial right up to the moment that his lips covered hers.

The warm, sensuous movement of his mouth drew a deep, almost feral moan that emanated from deep inside her as her lips parted. Her fingers closed around the fabric of his shirt as she raised herself up on her toes, her body stretching in a slim, urgent arc as she invited the invasion to deepen, expanding the cell-deep hungry ache until she simply hung on for the ride, helpless to resist the tide of attraction, the sparking electricity between them. She felt the deep quiver run through his body.

Then it was over. She wasn't quite sure how, but she was on her feet and not plastered up against him and he was standing there looking down at her as though… Actually, she wasn't sure he was seeing her at all. There was a hot blankness in his eyes that slowly receded.

'So what,' she began in a voice that really sounded nothing like her own, 'was that about?'

'Does the unknown that waits for you in there suddenly look so very scary?'

It didn't, but as explanations went that seemed more than thin. 'Why did you kiss me?'

Breathing hard, but looking insultingly composed considering the chaos inside her body and head, he brushed an invisible speck off his shirt before replying.

'A moment… I…I wanted to know how you tasted.'

The blunt words, drawn from him almost against his will, sent a slam of hot lust through her body.

CHAPTER NINE

'Oh!' Her response gave *inadequate* a new meaning, but she didn't know what else to say. What would be an improvement?

Don't do it again wouldn't be appropriate, or, more likely, *don't stop...*

'We'll be late.' Suddenly she was the one that couldn't hold *his* eyes.

'It's allowed—you're the guest of honour.' He dragged a hand over his dark hair, thinking about how warm and perfect she had felt in his arms. The promise of passion he had always sensed in her had burnt up into life the moment he'd touched her.

It was easy to see that Kat could become the drug of choice to any man, so long as he didn't mind sharing her with a multitude of good causes.

Theos, he really didn't envy that man!

Even as he congratulated himself he recognised that, but for the obligation he felt to Alekis, *he* would be that man, at least for a night, which was in itself another problem.

The insight he had gained into Kat's character led him to doubt that she had a casual attitude to sex. He doubted she would look on it as a healthy physical outlet. For her it would come wrapped up in sentiment. Of course, there were many men out there willing to accept those terms for the joy of bedding her.

Nothing of his thoughts showed in his face as they continued to walk side by side the last few yards, not touching, but he could still sense her leaping pulse.

'You'll be fine, you know.'

She gave an odd little laugh and lifted her head at the abrupt comment. 'Will I?' At that moment she didn't feel as if she knew anything. She ran her tongue across the outline of her lips and gave another laugh. Hell, she hadn't even known her own name when he'd kissed her.

'Be interested…' he said, the effort of dragging his eyes off her mouth making him sweat. 'Be yourself.'

Kat swallowed down another bubble of hysterical laughter. How was she meant to be *herself*, or even sane, after he had just kissed her like that? Being herself and kissing him back was part of the problem. *Herself* would be grabbing him and making him do it again.

'Now that is something I never thought I'd hear you say!' Wow, not even a quiver. She was extremely proud of herself.

He arched a sardonic brow. 'Why?'

'Because I get the impression me being me irritates the hell out of you tonight.' Maybe he had kissed her to shut her up, she thought, nursing her resentment.

He stopped short of the open door, from which the sounds of music and the hum of conversation and laughter emanated, and looked down at her.

'It isn't you I find—'

'Irritating?' she supplied, slightly confused and at the same time excited by the intensity in his manner, though next to the post-kiss confusion that still blocked her normal thought processes it barely even registered.

'Not the right word but it will do. It's the situation, Katina, that I find extremely…*irritating.*' *Theos*, wanting her was killing him.

'I don't know what you mean,' she said, thinking of the warm, clean but musky male smell of his body when he had kissed her. *Would he do it again?*

'Are you sure about that?'

She looked away, suddenly more nervous of the glow in his eyes than what lay in the room. Not nervous, excited. She ran her tongue across the dry outline of her lips. *It was just a kiss…stop trying to read things into it.*

She hefted out a deep sigh. 'Right, let's get this thing over with.'

He nodded.

She was incredibly glad for the light touch of his hand on her elbow as they walked into the room, because walking into a room beside Zach made it a dead certainty most of the room would not be looking at you. When Zach walked into a room, any room, he would always be the focus of attention.

There was a short static pause in the audible social hum as more and more people turned to look at them, from where they were already gathered in small groups, chatting, laughing, drinking the wine being offered by the staff.

The sea of faces was actually more a small pond, she told herself as she willed her feet that felt glued to the floor to move.

'Showtime, Kat.' He heard her whisper before flashing him a look from her topaz eyes and lifting her chin and walking away from him.

Zach watched her, while he wrestled with the flood of unfamiliar emotions surging inside him. He knew how scared she was but no one would ever have known it, despite her pallor, and even if they had it would have been her warmth they remembered, a warmth that could not be feigned.

He surprised himself with that thought.

He watched as she approached a man who stood

excluded from a small laughing group nearby. Zach's admiration and pride went through the roof as he watched her smile and move forward, touching the arm of the housekeeper before she lifted her head to the solitary man that Selene was offering the drink to.

Zach stood, his shoulder braced on one wall, his attitude possibly not as nonchalant as he intended because nobody approached him, not even one of the guys with the fizz, which was a pity because he could really have done with a drink.

He finally managed to grab one and downed it while fighting a strong urge to march over there and tell Kat that it didn't matter what anyone thought and this wasn't a test.

What the hell was wrong with Alekis, making her jump through all these hoops? And what was wrong with him for helping? If anyone needed to change it was them, not her.

He was shocked by this thought that came from he knew not where—unlike the urge to kiss her; that source was no mystery.

He willed himself to relax. He knew she could cope and so could he. He took a swallow and grimaced, finding he was holding an empty glass. If he could relive the moment…but he couldn't so why waste the energy? The kiss, while not being ideal, had at least taken the edge off his rampant hunger.

Yeah, you keep telling yourself that, Zach.

Tuning out the ironic voice of his subconscious, he watched as the austere diplomat melted under Kat's charm offensive and took a drink for himself before handing her the fruit juice option she must have requested. He saw her press a hand to her temple and carry on smiling… It was not the first time he had seen the gesture since she had begun to circulate.

The diplomat leaned in and said something that drew a laugh from Kat, a laugh so warm and spontaneous and *genuine* that it made other people smile, including him.

In the periphery Zach was aware of two people separate off from a nearby group and move to join Kat and the diplomat. One was a journalist that he didn't actively dislike, the other… He frowned as he recognised the other was Spiro Alekides, the business rival who had *not* been gracious in defeat and had made his humiliation worse by giving several unwise interviews that had harmed his reputation more than his financial losses.

Zach began to slowly weave his way through the jostle of bodies, not questioning or analysing the protective instincts that directed his feet.

Even without Zach's warning Kat would have summed up Spiro Alekides, who she had instantly recognised from his photo, in a heartbeat. She had encountered the type before. He smiled a lot, but not with his eyes, and tried very hard to say what he *thought* you wanted to hear.

'Oh, yes, I so agree all that talent out there is going to waste. It's not about charity, it's about investing in our future and the youth are our future.'

The man sounded as though he were reading the label on a packet of cereal, but Kat nodded, repressing a wince as the headache moved behind her eyes. Experience told her if she didn't take measures it would become a full-blown migraine and all that entailed—which was *just* what she didn't need.

'Not everyone understands that,' she said, thinking, *Like you,* before adding, 'Sorry, Mr—'

'Call me Spiro, my dear.'

'Spiro.'

The older man turned quite slowly, arranging his features into a smile. 'Why, Zach, what a nice surprise, meeting you here like this.' He beamed at Kat and the journalist and extended a well-manicured, plump hand to Zach, who raised both of his. One was holding a glass, the other a plate.

Zach smiled, making Kat think of a large sleek predator. She suspected that every woman present would have jumped straight into his mouth if the occasion arose—she had. The thought made her blush.

'So where is your lovely lady tonight?'

The reference to the woman that they had both slept with increased the tempo of the throb behind Kat's eyes. If she was going to get a migraine every time anyone mentioned a woman Zach had bedded she could spend her life with a headache!

'She couldn't make it.'

'Such a shame,' Zach murmured. 'Well, gentlemen, I hope you'll forgive me for stealing away our lovely hostess.' He planted a hand lightly in the small of Kat's back. 'But there is someone who is dying to meet her.'

Not happy that she liked the supportive feel of his hand as much as she did, she frowned and asked, 'Who?' without enthusiasm as they wove their way across the room.

'Do you have a headache?' Zach asked without looking at her.

Kat's jaw dropped and her eyes flew to his face, which sent a fresh spasm of agony along her nerve endings. *'How...?'*

His hand went to her elbow as she caught her heel in the hem of her dress and lurched. 'I thought as much,' he said grimly.

'What are we...?'

She stopped as he paused as they reached Selene and explained in an undertone, 'Kat has a headache. I'm taking her outside for some fresh air.'

'But you can't— This is— I have to stay. Some aspirin, Selene, and I'll be fine.'

'That too, please, Selene. You nearly passed out,' he condemned.

'For heaven's sake, I tripped, is all! It's the damned heels and don't blame me—you bought them for me! Not bought as such,' she tacked on hastily in case anyone had heard and got the wrong impression.

Zach stood over her as she swallowed the pain-killers and, ignoring his frowning disapproval, washed them down with a mouthful of wine.

'I thought you didn't drink.'

'A mouthful and, anyway, what did you *think* I was going to do—spit them out?' She took a deep breath and massaged her temples. 'OK, back to it.'

'You need some fresh air.'

She looked up at him, exasperated by his insistence. 'I need to get back in there.'

'They can wait.'

'Make up your mind. I thought this party was ultra-important…first impressions, burying bad news with my stunning personality, and all that stuff?'

'The pain is making you cranky. You need some fresh air to clear your head.'

She sighed. It was easier to give up, and the idea of escaping for a few moments had distinct appeal. The lively music the live band struck up made up her mind.

* * *

He didn't say anything until they got outside. 'So, you met Spiro.'

She inhaled as they stepped out into the scented night and she let her head fall back. 'Uh-huh, a real charmer, isn't he? If you go for snakes, that is.'

'Not a man to be underestimated, though.'

She lifted her head and walked alongside him onto the sloping lawns that ran down to the beach. The breeze tugged at her hair, dislodging several strands from her updo. She stuck them back in haphazardly.

'He is a poor loser. He takes pleasure from revenge…'

She flashed a look at his profile in the moonlight. 'What did he do?'

'He tried to sabotage something that is…important to me.'

It had taken a while to work out there was actually a pattern to the seemingly arbitrary flurry of false, damaging stories circulating online. The near career-ending false stories about abuse, about a dedicated and vital staff member at the charity for street kids that few knew had anything to do with Zach, and simultaneously the exposé about bullying in the mentoring scheme set up for teens emerging from care.

A firm specialising in forensic investigation had

taken about five minutes to reveal that the older man's grubby hands were all over the mess.

The threat of litigation had made the problem vanish. For good measure Zach had explained that he didn't need to resort to lies to bring Spiro down, and that he had in his possession several verifiable documents that would ensure the older man did jail time. As bluffs went it was a no-brainer. A man like Spiro always had dirty secrets.

'Your mentoring scheme for street kids, you mean.'

He stopped dead and looked at her in astonishment. 'How the hell do you know that?'

'What?' she said, dancing ahead and turning around to face him as she continued to skip backwards on her crazy high heels. 'That you are a bleeding heart do-gooder…?' she taunted, allowing herself a triumphant little laugh, frustrated that the shadows across his face meant she could only see his mouth, not his eyes. 'I talk to people. They open up to me. It's a gift.'

He swore.

'I don't know why you act like it's a dirty secret. I think it's marvellous!'

'You know nothing about me—the things I've—'

Her smile faded. 'I know you lived on the streets, and you survived.' That he'd had to protect himself and he had never learnt how to stop;

it wasn't a matter of didn't, he *couldn't* seem to open up to anyone.

'Selene?' he growled as he strode out at a pace that made her skip to keep up with him.

'Don't blame her, she assumed I knew already. You ran away from your uncle, the one who died?'

He nodded.

'And you never went back?'

His face was in shadow and when he finally responded his voice was wiped clean of all emotion as he reacted to the question. 'I went back looking for what... I suppose some sort of closure. He was gone. Dead, I found out later, and my grandmother...dementia, final stages.'

Kat gave a little gasp, feeling his pain as sharply as if it were her own as she fell into step beside him once more. 'What happened?'

'Nothing. I put her in a home and haven't been back since the first time.'

'So, she is having the best care?' It said so much about him that he would do that for someone who had abused him so badly.

'Oh, I can provide her with the best care, but I can't...*feel*...anything.'

She reached out in the dark and curled her small fingers around his. She could feel the raw tension emanating from him in waves. 'Sorry.'

'I suppose you think I should forgive her?' he flung out.

'No, I think that you should celebrate the day you escaped every year. I'll help you if you like?'

He looked down just as the moon came out from behind a cloud. It illuminated her beautiful face with breathtaking clarity, toasting her skin with moon gold.

CHAPTER TEN

HE STARED DOWN at her, drinking in each individual feature before gorging himself on the perfect whole. Then slowly, he lifted a hand and framed her face. Kat shivered at the contact and pushed her cheek against his hand, turning her face so that her lips brushed his palm.

His hand dropped.

'How will you help me?'

Her heart gave a painful jolt; her body was humming, her nerve endings raw as though all the insulation, the protection, had been stripped from them. 'I'd do anything you need,' she whispered.

A sound like a groan was torn from deep inside his chest. 'Don't say that, Katina.'

She lifted her chin. 'Why not?'

'Because I need everything.'

The heat between them scorched the air as he bent his head and kissed her. Kat kissed him back with equal abandon, locking her hands around his neck, arching her back to crush her breast into his chest, the little gasps of shocked pleasure as she felt the hardness of his desire against her belly lost in the warmth of his mouth.

They broke apart as the sound of a helicopter overhead cut through the sigh of the water.

Zach swore and took her hand. He studied it for a moment, an expression almost like pain contorting his features before his fingers tightened and he led her onto the moonlit sand.

Kat tripped.

'You're going to break your neck on those damned things. They are lethal.'

'But sexy.'

His eyes glowed hot and hungry. 'Hell, yes!'

The moonlight lent everything a silvered glow and the night-time silence made the hush of the waves breaking into a white foam hiss seem louder. There was no wind at all, just a warm stillness as, hopping on one foot and then the other, she whipped off the heels to walk beside him, her heart pounding in anticipation as they reached the point where the waves were breaking.

He turned, allowing himself to look at her. The fall had shaken free her hair from its elegant knot and it now spilled down her back and blew across her face in silky tangled strands that she pushed impatiently away with her free hand.

'I want to touch you.' He closed his eyes, trying

to get some sort of grip on the raw primal instincts that had him in a stranglehold. The muscles in his brown throat worked as he stared at her, but it was the heat in his passion-glazed eyes that made her insides dissolve and made her feet move of their own accord to close the distance between them.

Kat, her heart thudding, forgot what she was about to say, forgot how to speak, how to think; the raw need stamped into his strong, beautiful features thrilled through her and into a secret place nothing had ever penetrated before.

'This is a bad idea, Kat,' he slurred, struggling to think past the roar, the tidal wave of emotion rising inside him as he dragged a not quite steady hand through his hair.

'It's too late to go back,' she said, thinking, *In more ways than one,* as a surge of sheer hopeless longing made her tremble. He really was the epitome of male beauty as he stood there in the moonlight, his shirt open to the waist, his dark hair standing in sexy tufts, the shadow on his jaw and chin highlighting the angles and planes of his face.

'You're perfect,' she whispered, utterly dazzled by his perfection.

'Agape mou!' Zach looked into her eyes, saw the heat and hunger and felt his control burn away. It was impossible to tell who moved first but suddenly they were colliding, the impetus of the con-

tact driving the air out of her lungs; not that it mattered—Kat couldn't breathe anyway.

They sank to the sand together, lay side by side, thigh to thigh, for a moment breathing hard, staring into each other's eyes.

Zach moved first, reaching out to lay a big hand against her cheek, then, holding her gaze, he moved in with nerve-shreddingly slow deliberation to claim her trembling lips.

Kat's eyes squeezed closed as she focused on the taste of him, the feel of him, greedily absorbing the musky smell of his hard, male body mingled with the salty tang in the air.

The touch of his hand on one breast drew a soft feral whimper from her aching throat. She felt the air cool on her hot skin as he pushed the fabric away, revealing the turgid pink peak. The air around them crackled with the passion that burned away oxygen, leaving them in a bubble when, as if responding to some silent signal, they both began frantically tearing at each other's clothing, their mouths connected as they kissed with a wild lack of restraint, a desperate drowning feeling that Kat had never dreamt existed, let alone would ever feel.

Her entire body felt sensitised. She was aware of every touch, every abrasive point of friction between them and most of all the hot ache of arousal between her thighs.

Zach raised himself onto his knees, pulling Kat

with him, his lips not releasing hers for a second as his hands moved to the zip at the back of her dress. The need to see her was part of the madness consuming them both.

The dress slithered down to waist level.

Kat squeezed her eyes closed and felt, rather than heard, the vibration of his deep gasp, a gasp that was drowned out by her louder groan as she felt the touch of his mouth against the tip of one quivering soft breast and then the other. Her fingers speared into his dark hair, holding his head there against her to prolong this nerve-wrenching erotic sensation, giving herself over to the bliss.

By the time his head lifted, she was shaking everywhere and burning up. They faced one another, still kneeling as behind them the waves continued their relentless advance, retreat, hiss.

The pounding in Kat's blood did not retreat. It kept pushing forward, harder and harder, driving her deeper into the sensual maelstrom.

Zach leaned in to trail kisses down her neck, one hand cupping her breast, before pressing a fierce kiss to her parted lips.

'You feel like silk—so very soft,' he husked against her mouth.

'I want to feel...touch you...'

Their breath mingled, their tongues tangled as they continued to kiss with hungry, bruising intensity. Kat felt him quiver as she pushed aside the fabric of his shirt that hung open to allow her palms to slide down the smooth, slightly hair-roughened skin of his chest. She loved the feel of him, the hardness, the amazing definition of every individual ridge of muscle, every perfect contour. His skin felt fever hot under her exploring hands as he started to kiss down her body.

His tongue had found her nipple again when he felt the moment she encountered the scar, not from the knife but the surgical scar where they had opened his ribcage to save his life and massage his heart.

He lifted his head, the hot colour edging his cheekbones lending them a hard definition in the moonlight. Holding her eyes, he fought his way out of his shirt, allowing her to see the white line that ran midline along his breastbone and the more raised scar just under his ribs.

'What hap—?'

Her words were lost inside the possessive heat of his mouth as he pressed her back down onto the sand, the weight of his body pressing her deeper. The first skin-to-skin contact sent all questions, all thoughts from her head. She moved her hands over his broad shoulders, excited by his strength. The heat flaring between them as they continued to kiss and touch.

'Have you any idea how much I want you? Have wanted you from the first…the very first moment

I saw you?' The expression of fierce concentration on his face, the molten hunger in his eyes as he stroked a finger down her cheek as much as his erotic admission drew a throaty whimper from Kat's throat.

'I wanted you, too. Inside me. So much.'

The admission burned the remnants of his shredded control away; he gave a grin and levered himself off her.

He watched the protest die on her lips as she realised what he was doing; he was aware of her eyes following him as he unfastened his trousers and slid them down his thighs, kicking them away.

His boxers followed.

'Oh…!' She swallowed and felt the blood pool in the juncture between her legs. He really was magnificent, the level of his arousal was shocking, yet she wasn't embarrassed; his primitive male beauty fed the urgency in her blood.

She lay there, aching for his touch, and perhaps her desperation communicated itself because his hands moved down over the feminine curve of her hips as he freed her from the folds of dress fabric that had bunched across her. Her panties—scraps of lace—followed suit and he knelt back down beside her.

Kat reached out and touched him. He gasped and she felt him quiver as she stroked down the hot, hard length of him, then, emboldened, curved her fingers around him, touching the velvet tip with the pad of her thumb.

Nostrils flared, teeth clenched, he watched her, unable to tear his eyes from the expression of carnal concentration on her beautiful face. He bore it as long as he could before he grabbed her hand and, ignoring her protest, pushed her back, lowering his body onto her.

Hands held at the wrists above her head, all she could do at that first nerve-searingly perfect moment of skin-to-skin was moan. Then moan a lot more and squirm against him as she felt his hand slide between their bodies and in between her legs, exposing the heat in her sensitised core to his clever touch.

She tried to breathe, moving against the heel of his hand at the intimate exploration until it got so intense that she couldn't bear it. The pleasure moving close to the pleasure-pain line.

'Please,' she whispered, her teeth closing around the lobe of his ear. 'I can't...' she begged. 'It's too... You're too...'

'Relax, it's all right,' he slurred against her neck as he gave into the primal roar in his blood and parted her legs. 'Wrap your legs around me, hold me.'

She did, happy to take instruction. She was in uncharted territory, and he really seemed to know what he was doing. Zach was an intuitive, passionate and generous lover. She knew from conversations she had frequently felt excluded from that this was a rather rare combination.

She stopped thinking anything when he slid into her, his powerful thrust slowed by the tightness of her warm female body as it adjusted to him, relaxing and contracting as he began to touch deeper inside her, waking nerve endings that sent rush after rush of mindless bliss through her body.

'You feel…oh, Zach…you feel—' Her words were lost in the warm moisture of his mouth.

She felt as if she were on fire as she pushed towards an unseen goal and when she reached it the shock of release jerked her entire body as the pleasure spread from her scalp to her curling toes.

Her muscles had started to relax when she felt the hot rush of his climax; a moment later he rolled off her and they lay side by side, panting.

It felt like coming back to earth after floating far above it; it wasn't a thing that happened in a moment.

When she did Kat was smiling.

He watched as with fluid grace she rolled on her side, then he took her hand to kiss her open palm before he drew her warm, pliant body to him.

Relaxed… As it seeped through his body it took him a while to recognise the feeling. He did not associate sexual release with being relaxed; lowering your guard to that degree, opening yourself that much, required trust.

Then it hit him like a wall, the knowledge that scared him more than anything else could—in the few days he had known her she had burrowed her way through all the barriers he'd thrown up into his soul, his heart. If he loved her this much now, how much deeper, stronger would it grow if he let it?

How much harder it would be when it ended, when he let her down; there was a terrible inevitability to it. No one had ever been there for him and he had never been there for anyone else; a genetic flaw or something he'd never learnt, it remained a fact.

It was in his genes. Who would pass on a heritage like that? It would stop with him.

He closed his eyes and lay there, feeling her hands on his body, exploring. She was a giver and he was a taker, but he didn't have the will or the strength to stop her. He wanted the moment to last.

She watched Zach. He appeared to be sleeping, his breath even and steady, his chest rising and falling. The rest of him… Her glance slid lower and she blushed, remembering the pleasure his body had given her. The rest of him was perfect. The only flaw, if it could be counted as such, was the long surgical scar she had seen.

Zach tensed and kept his eyes closed as he felt

her fingers move down the scar on his chest; he'd known it was coming. In a moment she'd find the more messy, less surgically precise scars on his ribs, which the knife, luckily for him, had just glanced off, not penetrated. It was the one underneath that had thrust upwards, severing some major vessels, that had caused all the damage.

The only people who knew the truth of the scars were Alekis and Selene, plus the surgical team who had saved his life, the *real* heroes. He was indulgent of a little morbid curiosity from his bed partners. He even had a few ridiculous lies he wheeled out on occasion to amuse himself, safe in the knowledge they really didn't care about his pain or his trauma or the fact his uncle had knocked seven bells out of him—these were all pluses.

This was different. Kat's curiosity would not be morbid. Her empathy had quite a different quality and would include sympathy and pity, two things he had a strong allergic reaction to.

He opened his eyes and turned his head and, despite everything, experienced a shock-level surge of possessiveness as his eyes slid over her lovely face and beautiful body.

She smiled.

You made a mistake that was human and, if not, forgivable as such, but at least you could have a

*free pass; you repeated it and there were no free
passes because you were a fool.*

He was not a fool.

He'd made a mistake and he was not about to re-
peat it. This was going nowhere, because he didn't
do tomorrow and she very definitely did. The kind-
est thing in the long run—and she might appreciate
it one day, when she had her family and her brood
of children—was a clean cut. Not that there would
be anything clean about it if Alekis found out.

She had edged a little closer, planning to put
her head on his chest, pushing her long leg against
his hair-roughened thigh, enjoying the contrast in
their bodies. They were two very different halves
that had made a total perfect whole. At the last
moment something in his face, or rather the *lack*
of it, made her pause.

'Is something wrong?' Fear of losing this happiness made her tense.

'I didn't protect you.' The only time in his life.

It took a moment for his words and the self-
contempt in his voice to make sense.

'I'm sorry.'

'I was there, too,' she reminded him quietly. 'It
was my responsibility, too.'

He closed his eyes and shook his head. 'You
would say that.' Because she was good…too good
for him, but the truth was she had given and he
had taken.

She reached out again and touched the scar, pale against the deep gold of his skin. 'What happened?' she asked, her tender heart aching as she thought of the pain those marks represented.

He took her hand off his chest, dropped it as if it were something contagious and sat up. 'One of those "wrong place wrong time" things.'

She blinked and felt the trace of unease already stirring in her belly take serious hold. 'Is that all I get…?' She smiled to lighten her words and added half jokingly, 'You really could do with some lessons in sharing.'

He looked at her again; the coldness in his eyes made her stomach quiver in apprehension. She reached for her dress as the self-consciousness she had shrugged off returned. Pulling herself onto her knees, she slipped it over her head but didn't attempt the zip.

He didn't offer so she knelt back down again.

'We are not sharing, Katina. Yes, we had sex, but it was not the beginning of some special sharing, caring relationship. But if you want to know, the scars are why I am who I am. I was in the wrong place but so was Alekis.'

'You saved him.'

'I am not a hero, Kat. Do not look at me that way. I hate bullies and I didn't think before I acted…much like tonight.'

It wasn't just what he said, it was the fact he seemed to *want* to hurt her.

'You sound as though you regret it.'

She left him the space to say no, that it had been one of the best things that had ever happened to him, but the space stayed empty and instead his eyes drifted away from hers as if the contact was something that made him uncomfortable. 'It was a mistake—you must see that.'

Kat said nothing. She was actually afraid if she tried to speak she'd start crying.

'For starters, Alekis trusted me. I have betrayed that trust and betrayed someone I respect.' *But, man, is he good to hide behind.* Ignoring the sly insert of his subconscious, he appealed for her understanding. 'You must see that.'

'Why should I care about what Alekis thinks?' she flared back. 'Anyway, what about me? Don't I deserve a little bit of respect?' she choked out.

'Please do not become emotional…'

'*Seriously!* We just made love.'

'Had sex.'

The rebuttal made her pale.

'And do not imagine this is the start of some sort of love affair.'

She sat there shivering while he got to his feet and dragged his clothes on. There was a pause before he extended his hand to her; she ignored it and got to her feet.

'I know you want a happy-ever-after thing, a husband and children, which is fine, but I'm not the man for that and if I'd known you were so inexperienced I would have—' Innate honesty made him pause. If he'd known he would not have stopped—nothing would have stopped him.

'Don't put me in one of your little boxes, and don't presume to know what I want from life! You know something, Zach, I really don't think *I'm* the one with the problem. I didn't expect you to declare undying love. I just wanted a little bit of...well, respect would have been nice. But no, you had to spoil what happened by turning it into something nasty and sordid, because you're too scared to risk feeling anything that you can't control. You know what I think?'

His jaw clenched as he struggled to control his anger. 'Is there any way I can stop you telling me?'

'You won't have any sort of a future until you come to terms with your past and stop letting it rule you.'

'Who's presuming now?' he growled out.

She picked up her skirts in one hand, decided not to look for her shoes—they had killed anyway—and started back across the sand toward the lights of the house.

Zach, who experienced a stab of visceral longing as he watched her progress, dignified despite the fact her entire back, including the upper slopes of her pert bottom, was exposed, managed to wipe his face of expression as she suddenly swung back, her anger cancelling out mental censorship as she had the last word.

'You're not the only one with trust issues, Zach. Why the hell do you think I was inexperienced? Though, for the record, I was a virgin! And as it turns out a stupid one because I thought I had found someone I could let my guard down with. You know what, though, I'd prefer to be me and make a mistake than you, who spends his life pretending you don't feel anything...' Her eyes searched his face. 'But I don't believe that—you did and for me!'

The level of his self-loathing went up several notches as he watched her flounce away.

CHAPTER ELEVEN

'How did it go?'

Selene saw Kat's face and her own melted into one of concern. 'Oh, dear, is it bad news?'

Kat shook her head as she laid her handbag down on the table and turned back to the house-keeper. 'No, no, nothing like that really.' She was not ready to share just yet what the *something* was that had put the worried look on her face. 'The doctors are really pleased with his progress. If all goes well with his next round of tests, they are willing to discharge him next week.'

Kat was visiting the clinic in Athens once a week, but talking to her grandfather during the week online. This time she had taken herself off to see another specialist after seeing her grandfather.

'Things are definitely getting more relaxed.'

'He must be pleased he's coming home.'

'No, he's mad as hell that he can't escort me to this charity auction.'

'Never mind, there's next year.'

'That's what I said only he…yes, thanks, tea would be lovely,' she said with gratitude to a maid who brought in a tea tray.

'Only?'

'He has roped in a stand-in. He says as he has donated a sports car, an Azaria should be there. I said I'm not an Azaria but, well…' She shrugged. She had discovered her grandfather was a hard man to argue with and when faced with a defeat he fell back on chest pain, and who was going to risk disbelieving him?

Not Kat.

'Join me,' Kat begged when the woman poured her tea.

Smiling, Selene poured another and took a seat. 'So who is the stand-in? Anyone we know?'

Selene had already guessed, the way she had figured out at least some of what had gone on between Zach and Kat.

'Zach,' Kat said quietly. Unlike for Selene, the news had come as a massive shock when Alekis had announced his stand-in for the charity auction.

Kat had excused herself and gone to the ladies' room to cry her eyes out, but then she had an excuse for being over-emotional. Her hormones were all over the place—she was pregnant.

She'd had her suspicions for a few days and the consultant had officially confirmed it today.

To keep things private—the island was a very

small place—she'd asked Sue to post her the test kit. Her friend had been sympathetic but she had promised her that *nobody* knew that early, but Kat had, and she'd been right.

Two weeks to the day since Zach had left, never, it seemed, to return, she knew she was carrying his child. The shock was still there, even the occasional moment of blind panic, but a level of acceptance had started to kick in and, to her surprise, *excitement*.

While her emotions were all over the place, she was totally sure of one thing. This baby would have a mother who loved her or him. Her baby would never feel alone and be scared. She was absolutely determined to give this child the childhood she had not had.

Sadly, she could not guarantee the baby a father. And the great-grandfather? Well, the jury was still out, but she suspected, hoped, that Alekis would be over the moon about having a great-grandchild.

And if he wasn't, well, she would deal with it. The baby came first as far as she was concerned and if other people had a problem with that—tough!

It was the father's identity her grandfather might have a problem with. It was a problem the father himself might have, too. She had lain awake half of last night trying to decide when and how to tell Zach and had come to the conclusion that she needed to get used to the idea herself before she shared.

It made sense.

Or she might just be a big coward!

'It's a really stunning event with the cream of society and—'

'But Zach…' Kat wailed, still blaming her hormones.

Kat had taken to her room and cried for a day when Zach had left, claiming a migraine, and when she had emerged she had known that Zach wasn't the only person in denial.

Hard enough to accept she had wanted him physically, but accepting that she had fallen in love with Zach had been one of the hardest things in her life. She prided herself on being truthful but this was one truth she had been avoiding because she had known it would hurt—she just hadn't known how much!

'You could make an excuse…'

Kat's chin went up. 'Why should I?' She wasn't the one who had done anything wrong.

Zach, drawing eyes and more than a few camera clicks in his dress suit, stepped back into the shadows, and the limo that drew up disgorged the members of a new girl-band group.

The paparazzi went crazy and Zach's patience

grew thin. His offer to travel over to Tackyntha to escort Kat had been politely refused by someone who was not Kat or even Selene.

He was being given the runaround. The only surprise was that nothing of what had happened between he and Kat seemed to have filtered through to Alekis as yet.

The past two weeks had been a sort of hell Zach had never experienced before. Normally in times of stress he was able to bury himself in work until it passed, but not on this occasion. He couldn't concentrate, a unique experience for him, so work was impossible.

His volatile mood had swung from anger and frustration—he hadn't asked for any of this—and then on to black despair. It was crazy but he was missing her, not just the physical stuff, although that had been incredible, but stupid things like the sound of her voice…her laugh, the way she wrinkled up her nose.

The woman was haunting him.

Logic told him that a man couldn't fall in love so quickly, but the same logic told him that love, the romantic variety, didn't exist outside romance novels.

He'd believed that before Katina had walked into his life.

And now? Now he didn't know what the hell he felt, and her words kept coming back to him. *'You won't have any sort of a future until you come to terms with your past.'*

He was the one with the problem.

It still made him angry, but Zach had started to wonder if she could be right.

He had rejected the idea that he was a coward hiding behind his past and unable to face the future, but the more he thought about it… Tonight would give him a chance to connect again. Maybe there was some sort of middle ground?

He dashed a hand across his head. *Middle ground?* What the hell was he thinking?

He was thinking of kissing her—just sinking into her warmth—as he had been from the second she had walked away from him. He had struggled not to run after her. He had begun to wonder what would have happened if he had—maybe their passionate affair would already have burnt itself out?

Or she might have killed him.

A half-smile on his lips, he stepped forward again. This time the limos had arrived in a block of three.

The door to the first opened and a platinum blonde got out, wearing a glittery silver dress that was so figure-hugging it appeared painted on. She rocked a little on her heels as she paused to pose for cameras even though no one seemed that excited about her and her escort's arrival.

'Well, I hear that Alekis's little heiress will be

here tonight. I wonder if she's as much of a slut as the mother was.'

'Was she?' the man asked.

'God, yes, and a druggie… I hear that the girl is just like her. Alekis found her in some sort of refuge and I hear that before that she was actually living on the streets.'

The woman with the uniquely unattractive voice had begun talking as she emerged from the car. Standing at the top of a long flight of stone steps, Zach nonetheless heard every word of this conversation.

He stepped in front of the doormen.

The woman looked him up and down, her painted lips widening into a smile. 'Oh, hello, how nice to see you again, Zach. Darling, it's Zach.'

Zach, who had not to his knowledge ever seen either of them before, waited until she had finished listing to her long-suffering partner all the times they had met him previously.

'I heard you speaking—actually I think several people heard you speaking—about Miss Katina Parvati,' Zach observed, pitching his own voice to carry. It was a message he did not mind sharing. 'I did not like what I heard. Obviously anyone with an ounce of sense will recognise spiteful lies and malice when they hear it. But I feel it only fair to warn you that should I hear those lies repeated anywhere online or in person I will have no compunction but to put the case in the hands of my *very* litigious legal team. And after they have finished with you I am sure that Alekis Azaria might enjoy watching his own team picking at your bones. His granddaughter is a person so superior to the likes of you that I find it offensive that you breathe the same air!'

'Zach!'

At the sound of the voice he turned. Kat was standing at the bottom of the steps, wearing a dress a shade paler than the one he remembered stripping off her body. This one was much more formal: a strapless bodice that revealed the upper slopes of her breasts and the dazzle of a diamond necklace.

He rushed down to her, taking the steps two at a time, shedding his doubts with each step he took. What he felt for her was not going to burn itself out. She was part of him and if he ever won her back he would never let her go!

'Do you make a habit of making public scenes?' Oh, God, he looked so gorgeous she could not take her eyes off him. The ache of longing she had struggled to deny was a physical ache that went soul deep.

He looked blank for a moment, a little dazed, and then glanced up the stairs. The couple had vanished.

'Not usually.' His shoulders lifted in a shrug.

There was so much he needed to say but now

she was here and he was acting like some tongue-tied kid, or maybe just the Neanderthal who had taken her virginity on a beach she probably thought he was.

Kat lowered her eyes and struggled to collect her fractured composure. Seeing him standing there had shaken loose a million conflicting emotions. The idea that she could distance herself from him emotionally or any other way had vanished.

He was the father of her child and she loved him.

'I heard what you said,' she said, not even bothering to try and project the illusion of calm control—who was going to believe it? 'I think maybe a lot of people did.'

That was the problem: there were way too many people and he wanted her all alone. 'Let's get this over with,' he said, taking her elbow and mentally figuring out just how soon they could reasonably leave without causing massive offence. While he had zero problem with offence, he suspected that Kat might not be on the same page as him with this.

'You've not lost any of your charm,' she said, hating the fact he had the ability to hurt her.

He looked down at her, frowning. 'No, I didn't mean… I need to talk to you alone and I avoid these things like the plague normally.'

Warning herself not to read anything into his

words or the possessive blaze in his eyes when he looked at her, she allowed herself to be escorted into the room.

Selene had warned her that everyone crowded into the small space for drinks and finger food before the auction, which was to be held in the marquee outside. And it was crowded, very! The jewels she had been so reluctant to wear were not the most extravagant baubles on display. Kat had never seen so much bling in such a small space in her life, though maybe the impression was exaggerated because the walls felt as if they were closing in on her.

'Fruit juice, please,' she said as she was offered champagne. 'I feel like everyone is staring at me.'

'They are. You're the most beautiful woman in the room.'

It might have given her more pleasure to hear him say this had her head not started to spin in a really sickening fashion. She lifted her head as the lights above began to blur.

'Zach?'

He caught her before she hit the floor and when she opened her eyes, he was kneeling beside her looking pale while he emptied the contents of her small bag onto the floor.

'Where's the EpiPen…? Does anyone have an EpiPen? This is anaphylactic shock. Will someone call an ambulance?'

'No, Zach, it isn't.'

A look of intense relief washed over his face. *'Agape mou*...no, don't move, you fainted. I think you might have eaten something with peanuts in.'

'No, I haven't.' She hadn't eaten a thing; she'd been too nervous about tonight. 'You remembered!'

'I remember every word you have ever said to me.'

She ran her tongue over her dry lips and tried to lift her head. 'No, stay there, wait for the ambulance.' A large hand on her chest made it impossible for her to defy this edict.

'Will you stop it?' she said, batting his hand with both hers. 'I'm not ill, you idiot, I'm pregnant!'

Her exported admission coincided with a lull in the conversation that had started up when people had guessed she wasn't dead. The room had excellent acoustics so at least eighty per cent of the people present heard the happy news.

Beside her, Zack had frozen. The blood had quite literally drained from his face; he looked much more in need of an ambulance than she did.

'Pregnant.'

She nodded.

A long sibilant hiss left his lips as he leaned back onto his heels.

'Only just...obviously.'

His hand lifted from her chest, but her relief was

short-lived. He needed both hands to scoop her up and carry her out of the place, magnificently oblivious to the hundred pairs of eyes watching them.

Outside, a car appeared as if by magic. Zach slid her into the back seat as if she were a piece of porcelain before joining her.

'I don't know… I don't know what to say.' His dark eyes slid to her belly. 'You're sure?'

She nodded. 'Sorry.'

His dark brows lifted. 'Do not say sorry. A child is, is…' A child was scary. 'A blessing. At least that was what one of the nuns who taught me in kindergarten said. I think she decided I was an exception when I asked her how many she had.'

'You don't have to pretend, Zach,' she said, sounding understanding but feeling miserable as hell. If he could allow himself to love her even half as much as she loved him, they could have a wonderful life. A family, because, even if he did not know it, she knew he was a marvellous man who had overcome more than most people could imagine. 'I know that this is the very last thing you would have wanted and I'm not going to ask you for anything.'

'You shouldn't have to ask.' He stared at her for a moment before giving a cracked laugh. 'And you don't have to. Obviously, we're getting married.'

It was Kat's turn to laugh. 'Is that meant to be funny?'

'You tried telling Alekis that yet?'

'This is nothing to do with Alekis.'

Rather to her surprise, Zach nodded. 'No, it isn't.' He leaned forward and lifted a hank of hair from her face, tucking it behind her ear with such tenderness that it brought tears to her eyes. 'I came here tonight wanting to talk to you, to say some things. How about I do that first and then we talk about…?' His eyes dropped, a smile curving his lips, as her hand lifted to cover the flatness of her belly protectively.

'So you don't want to discuss the elephant in the room.'

'I want very much to discuss it, but there are things I need to say first to put what has happened into perspective. Would that be okay with you?'

She nodded warily and glanced at the partition between them and the driver.

'He can't hear us.'

'All right.'

'Firstly, you were right. I do have a problem. The past is…has been stopping me moving on. I've been alone for a long time and I decided that was a strength, but I realise now that it is in fact a weakness.'

'It's lonely,' she said quietly, her heart aching for the lonely boy he'd been. 'I know. It's not weak, Zach, it's just…sometimes you need to give a bit of yourself to get something back.' Kat knew she'd been lucky she'd had foster parents who had taught her that. Zach had had no one; he'd been alone.

'It's *easier* to be alone,' he said with a self-recriminatory grimace. 'I was willing to walk away from the best thing that ever happened to me because I was scared. A coward. I've been wrong about a lot of things in my life but this here with you… I was insane to let you walk away.'

'You didn't let me walk, Zach, you threw me away.'

A look of shame crossed his face as he heard the bitterness in her voice. 'You're right. I'm an idiot. I think that part of me cannot believe that I am allowed to be happy in that way—to have something so precious and lose it… I think that was my fear. I was afraid that I couldn't look after you like I couldn't look after my mother.'

Heart aching for the pain drawn on his face, she caught his hand and pressed it between both of her own. 'You were a child, Zach. It wasn't your job to do the looking after.'

'Being alone was my way of feeling in charge… but I'm not going to think of being alone now, and I'm going to think of that time when I was as the time I was waiting for you, until that moment I saw you, in that graveyard, looking like a sexy angel.'

'There was someone there!' she breathed, recalling the day when she had sensed a presence as she'd laid flowers at her mother's grave.

He gave a half-smile. 'I couldn't get your face out of my head.' He took his phone from his pocket and showed her the snapshot. 'Have you any idea how many times a day I have looked at that?'

The tears that had filled Kat's eyes as he spoke spilled out, sparkling on her lashes. 'You're not saying this just because of the baby? I really couldn't bear that.'

'The baby... Now that is something I never thought I would have, but now I am claiming it.' He pressed a possessive hand to her stomach and his mouth to her lips.

The kiss was deep and tender and life-affirming.

'I love you, Kat!' Just saying it felt liberating, so he said it again, aching sincerity throbbing in his voice. 'I love you and I hope you will one day learn to love me. Marry me, Kat. Let us be a family.'

'That's not possible, Zach, because I'm already totally insanely in love with you!' she cried, throwing her arms around his neck.

EPILOGUE

'I WANT TO see the person in charge!'

Kat's eyes lifted from the baby in her arms to see her handsome husband standing at the side of the bed.

'He is just so perfect…yes, I think Alek suits him?' Her husband looked as exhausted as she had felt, but it was a good tired that came with a deep feeling of contentment.

'I think so. You should really get some sleep, you know.'

She nodded. 'We have a family, Zach.' There was wonder in her face as she looked down at the baby who had arrived at six that morning.

Zach covered her hand with his own. 'We are a family,' he corrected, looking deep into her eyes.

The bellowing voice interrupted the tender moment, making itself heard once more. This time the baby's eyes opened; they were dark, flecked with amber.

'Hush, Alek, we will not let Great-Grandpa wake you up. You'll get used to him.'

'If he's anything like his mother he'll have the old man wrapped around his little finger in no time at all.'

'What can I say?' Kat said with a smile. 'I'm irresistible. You know, you really *should* go and tell him to come in. You know he's creating havoc out there.'

Zach gave a resigned sigh and levered himself off the bed, pausing to touch the dark head of his son and press a warm kiss to his wife's lips. 'You did good, kid.'

'A joint effort,' she protested.

'Hardly. My contribution required much less effort,' he said with the wicked grin she loved so much.

'Oh, I helped a little bit with that too, as I recall.'

His grin deepened. 'Well, I have to say I'm really relieved he doesn't look like Alekis. That was my secret fear all along.'

'Oh, was that what your secret fear was?' she teased lovingly. 'I thought it was I might slip, I might get too hot, I might get too cold, I might—'

'All right, all right, a man is allowed to be protective, isn't he? And now we have this… He is very beautiful, isn't he?'

'Of course he is, he looks just like his papa.'

'Doctor!' the voice outside thundered scornfully. 'I wish to speak to the person in charge, not a child.'

'Oh, really, Zach, go and give him the news before he starts telling everyone how there would be no baby if he hadn't thrown us together, and that it was all part of his grand plan…' She broke off and gave a laugh of delight as the baby's tiny perfect fingers curled around one of her own. 'He is so strong, aren't you, my precious?' She looked up. 'You don't think there was a grand plan, do you?'

'You know something, *agape mou*? I really don't care. I am here with you and our baby. I don't care if the devil himself arranged it. I am just happy.'

Kat nodded. 'Me too.' She lifted a hand to stifle a yawn. 'Tired and happy.'

The addition made him smile. 'Right, I will go and tell your grandfather that you are not allowed visitors until tomorrow.'

'But the midwife said—'

Zach kissed her to silence. 'Tomorrow.'

'You are a very good husband.'

'I am a work in progress, but my heart,' he promised, pressing his hand first to his own chest and then against Kat's beating heart, 'is definitely in it.'

'Seen the name outside the surgical wing, young man? That is *my* name. I think you'll find I have some influence in this place!' Alekis shouted from the hallway.

'But he doesn't in this room,' Kat promised the sleeping baby in her arms.

Zach nodded his agreement. 'Oh, everyone at

the refuge sent their love when I texted the news. Sue made a flying visit to the new refuge and she said to tell you there were no problems.'

'Oh, that is good news!' In the months after they had joined forces there had been five more refuges opened and Zach's mentoring scheme had started up in two UK cities.

'She also says everything is under control, so relax and enjoy the baby.'

'I—' Kat broke off as a loud bellow outside made the sleeping baby stir. 'Go and save the poor staff, Zach.'

Laughing, he obeyed, because after all Kat had saved him from a lonely life. She had given him the greatest gift there was—unconditional love.

* * * * *

If you enjoyed
A Passionate Night with the Greek
*You're sure to enjoy these other stories
by Kim Lawrence!*

A Ring to Secure His Crown
The Greek's Ultimate Conquest
A Cinderella for the Desert King
A Wedding at the Italian's Demand

Available now

#3749 THE GREEK'S VIRGIN TEMPTATION
by Susan Stephens
Jilted bride Kimmie is adamant that her honeymoon party will still go ahead. Her celebration leads her to billionaire Kristof...who tempts Kimmie to share her unspent wedding night with him!

#3750 SHOCK MARRIAGE FOR THE POWERFUL SPANIARD
Conveniently Wed!
by Cathy Williams
Rafael has one aim: to find Sofia—the woman due to inherit the company he's poised to take over—and propose a mutually beneficial marriage! But this Spaniard's potent need for Sofia is unexpected—and changes everything...

#3751 IRRESISTIBLE BARGAIN WITH THE GREEK
by Julia James
Heiress Talia is stunned when Luke, the stranger she spent one earth-shattering night with, returns! He offers Talia a job to save her family home... She can't turn down the arrangement—or deny their still-powerful chemistry!

#3752 REDEEMED BY HER INNOCENCE
by Bella Frances
Ruthless Nikos won't risk his company to save Jacquelyn's struggling bridal boutique. But he will give her the best night of her life! Could untouched Jacquelyn's sensual surrender be this dark-hearted Greek's redemption?

HPCNM0819RB

Get 4 FREE REWARDS!

We'll send you 2 FREE Books
<u>plus</u> 2 FREE Mystery Gifts.

Harlequin Presents® books feature a sensational and sophisticated world of international romance where sinfully tempting heroes ignite passion.

FREE Value Over **$20**

YES! Please send me 2 FREE Harlequin Presents® novels and my 2 FREE gifts (gifts are worth about $10 retail). After receiving them, if I don't wish to receive any more books, I can return the shipping statement marked "cancel." If I don't cancel, I will receive 6 brand-new novels every month and be billed just $4.55 each for the regular-print edition or $5.80 each for the larger-print edition in the U.S., or $5.49 each for the regular-print edition or $5.99 each for the larger-print edition in Canada. That's a savings of at least 11% off the cover price! It's quite a bargain! Shipping and handling is just 50¢ per book in the U.S. and $1.25 per book in Canada.* I understand that accepting the 2 free books and gifts places me under no obligation to buy anything. I can always return a shipment and cancel at any time. The free books and gifts are mine to keep no matter what I decide.

Choose one: ☐ **Harlequin Presents®**
Regular-Print
(106/306 HDN GNWY)

☐ **Harlequin Presents®**
Larger-Print
(176/376 HDN GNWY)

Name (please print)

Address   Apt. #

City   State/Province   Zip/Postal Code

> Mail to the **Reader Service:**
> **IN U.S.A.:** P.O. Box 1341, Buffalo, NY 14240-8531
> **IN CANADA:** P.O. Box 603, Fort Erie, Ontario L2A 5X3

Want to try 2 free books from another series? Call 1-800-873-8635 or visit www.ReaderService.com.

---

*Terms and prices subject to change without notice. Prices do not include sales taxes, which will be charged (if applicable) based on your state or country of residence. Canadian residents will be charged applicable taxes. Offer not valid in Quebec. This offer is limited to one order per household. Books received may not be as shown. Not valid for current subscribers to Harlequin Presents books. All orders subject to approval. Credit or debit balances in a customer's account(s) may be offset by any other outstanding balance owed by or to the customer. Please allow 4 to 6 weeks for delivery. Offer available while quantities last.

Your Privacy—The Reader Service is committed to protecting your privacy. Our Privacy Policy is available online at www.ReaderService.com or upon request from the Reader Service. We make a portion of our mailing list available to reputable third parties that offer products we believe may interest you. If you prefer that we not exchange your name with third parties, or if you wish to clarify or modify your communication preferences, please visit us at www.ReaderService.com/consumerschoice or write to us at Reader Service Preference Service, P.O. Box 9062, Buffalo, NY 14240-9062. Include your complete name and address.

HPI9R3

Rum distiller Kitty is shocked to learn that César,
the elusive stranger she shared one explosive night with,
is actually her boss. But that's nothing compared to
Kitty's latest realisation… She's pregnant!

Read on for a sneak preview of
Louise Fuller's next story for Harlequin Presents,
Consequences of a Hot Havana Night.

She looked up at César. "It's positive."

His expression didn't change by so much as a tremor.

"I'm pregnant."

She knew that these tests were 99 percent accurate, but somehow saying the words out loud made it feel more real. It was there—in her hand. She was going to have a baby.

Only, the person who was supposed to be the father, supposed to be there with her, was no longer around.

Her heartbeat had slowed; she felt as if she was in a dream. "I'm pregnant," she said again.

César's grip tightened around her hand, and as she met his gaze she felt her legs wilt. His eyes were so very green, and for a moment all she could think was that they should be brown.

Her head was swimming. It had taken five years, but most days she was content with her life. She still regretted Jimmy's death, but the acute pain, that hollowed-out ache of despair, had faded a few years ago. Only now this news had reawakened old emotions.

He caught her arm. "You need to sit down."

Still holding her hand, he led her into the living room. She sat down on the sofa. The first shock was starting to wear off and panic was starting to ripple over her skin.

"I don't understand how this could happen."

When she and Jimmy had started trying for a baby, he had been so keen he'd taken a fertility test and everything had been normal. She'd been about to get herself checked out when he fell ill, and then there had been too much going on, other more urgent tests to take, and so each time she wasn't pregnant she had blamed herself—her periods had always been irregular. Only now it seemed as though it hadn't been her.

César sat down beside her. "I'm pretty sure it happened the usual way."

She stared at him dazedly. Her head was a muddle of emotions, but he was so calm. So reasonable.

"You haven't asked me," she said slowly, "if the baby could be someone else's."

In a way, that was more of a shock than her pregnancy. With hindsight, her late period, her sudden craving for fruit juice and her heightened relentless fatigue all pointed to one obvious explanation, but she knew it was a question most men in his situation would have asked.

He leaned back a little, studying her face. There was an expression in his eyes that she couldn't fathom.

For a moment he didn't reply, and then he shrugged. "What happened between us isn't something I've found easy to forget. I'd like to believe that you feel the same way. But if you think there's any question over my paternity, now would be a good time to say so."

She shook her head. "There hasn't been anyone but you." Her eyes flicked to his face. "And, yes, I feel the same way."

As she spoke, some of the tension in her shoulders lifted. They hadn't planned for this to happen, to bring new life into the world, and they might not love one another, but those few heated moments had been fierce and important for both of them, and she was glad that this child had been conceived out of such extraordinary mutual passion.

"I don't regret it," she said abruptly. "What we did or what's happened."

Her heart swelled. She had wanted and waited for this baby for so long, and suddenly all those other tests, with their accusatory ghostly white rectangles, seemed to grow vague and unsubstantial.

"Well, it's a little late for regrets." He paused. "This baby isn't going anywhere. What matters now is what happens next."

Don't miss
Consequences of a Hot Havana Night
available September 2019 wherever
Harlequin® Presents books and ebooks are sold.

www.Harlequin.com